. . . but to you I'll stay forever true!

New Year's Eve

Clock goes Big Bang
while space stays silent:

Time with a twang
meets magic island.

. . . but to you I'll stay forever true!

A Heart Therapy-Blog

*Viable pathways,
cul-de-sacs or dead end roads
and common sense solutions
in the labyrinth of psychotherapy*

Tales from the therapy room
by
Gabriele Breucha & Anselm Keussen

Imprint

Bibliographical information
of the German National Library:
The German National Library lists this
publication in the German National Bibliography.
Detailed bibliographic data is available on the Internet at
http://dnb.dnb.de

Authors: **Gabriele Breucha & Anselm Keussen**
©opyright 2025 Dr. med. Anselm Keussen

Publisher: **BoD · Books on Demand** GmbH, In de Tarpen 42,
22848 Norderstedt, bod@bod.de
Print: Libri Plureos GmbH, Friedensallee 273,
22763 Hamburg
ISBN: 978-3-7693-0762-7
Available as paperback and e-book at:
https://www.bod.de/buchshop

Please note: The information in this book has been
researched and compiled as carefully as possible.
However, no guarantee can be given for any of the
contents published in this text.

Imprint continued

Please note that the term: **unconscient** is used in this text - instead of the words: *un-* or *subconscious* - to describe processes in our personality, which are most of the time happening in parallel or 'below' our *waking consciousness.*

Our **unconscient** houses major parts of our mind or psyche, which usually are accessible only in dreams, during hypnosis - or whenever our more outward oriented 'knowing mind' shifts in the direction of our wider and *inner awareness.*

PS:
Brevity is the spice of life
Almost all tasks that can be solved in a short time can also be worked through in a much longer time.

Contents

A comprehensive table of contents that allows you to navigate to all the subsections directly.

Poems:

True. A foreword

There is more going on in families
than meets the eye.
Virginia Satir
American family therapist

Dear reader,
with this, we greet you in our essay on some hopefully innovative methods in present as well as future psychotherapy, psychosomatic medicine and psychiatry.

First about the structure of this essay: People who are in psychotherapy or who intend to do so almost always are suffering from internal loyalty conflicts - for example between their parents back then and their partners and children today.

Therefore, dealing with these sometimes very stressfully ambivalent loyalties of the patients is one of the central levels in this summary of anecdotal stories from the therapy room.
This also includes this strange sentence on the subject of 'true and new', which you may have noticed already on the title and back page of this book.
But 'true' is a good thing, isn't it?, one might object.

And that's right, of course, because the 'true soul' and the 'true guy' are faithful, which means, they are reliable, loyal in their partnership and truthful.

Conflicts from early bonds of loyalty

This loyalty of character, however, which is so desirable in itself, can cause problems later in life if it was imprinted in difficult ways, during childhood or adolescence.

And this ambivalent imprinting, often burdened with shame and guilt, frequently results in entangled and pathologically loyal relations, in which depraved, frustrated and desperate adults - mostly parents, but also others from family, school, neighbourhood or church - meet children or adolescents or other people in their protection, who are then 'expected to help' those adults in their suffering.

And those children or people depending on the adults go along with this, partly out of ignorance, partly out of fascination with the erotic partnership role assigned to them, but above all, especially between parents and children, in order to stabilise the parents' partnership and thus the family.

In the following descriptions of some individual therapy processes, which are inspired by the experiences with our patients, we will go into more detail about how these supportive actions for confused and constantly stressed adults ultimately affect those children later on in their life.

A global error in programming our brains

These early traumatic encounters suffered by children as a result of inappropriate relationships offered by transgressing adults represent one of the worst global epidemics or programming errors that causes suffering for people and humanity, from the Stone Ages to Antiquity and from Renaissance to the Moon Shot and beyond.

The following, entirely fictional stories from the therapy room offer some possible solutions to this dilemma.

These early injuries to the child that are caused by abusive thoughts or actions of frustrated adults are almost always 'forgotten' due to feelings of shame and guilt and therefore repressed into the *unconscient* parts of the personality.

This is happening, because the child has often been told: 'But you mustn't tell anyone about that, and especially not . . . because they wouldn't understand.
It's our secret!'

Family secrets and their consequences
Unfortunately, these secrets leave wounds and scars in the child's psyche, which can impair the ability to say 'you' in an open way, to share closeness with others and especially to share and enjoy a free-flowing and loving intimacy with a partner later in life.

The pivotal word 'I-Thou'

It is precisely because they lost the basic word *'I-Thou'* in the sense of **Martin Buber** to such an extent that most people seek help in psychotherapy.
Because most people are yearning deeply for a genuine and successful contact with the 'you', both with the great 'Thou' that keeps the world going and whispers in our hearts, but also with the 'you' at eye level in a mutually supportive and loving partnership.

The work in therapy
Accordingly, psychotherapy in many cases is a working process that is step for step enabling the patient to improve and heal these wounds from childhood and adolescence to such an extent that - instead of symptomatic depressive moods, delusional ideas, panic attacks, fears or compulsions - a genuine, fundamental contact from 'I to You' is finally possible again on all levels.

Quite a challenge, and therefore we should right from the start be grateful for any developmental steps - even smaller ones - during the therapy process.

This is especially true because these so-called 'warlike conflicts' in families, in which adults 'take away their children's property' - in the sense of **Arno Gruen** - are harming humanity since prehistoric times already.

Injuries across the generations

These cascades of abuse from generation to generation, mostly by confused men, but frequently also by lonely women, which amount to intra-family wars, should be understood in their overall social and historical context.

From war to war

Doing so it soon becomes clear that it is those constant 'compensating' wars between traumatised and ego-enslaved men that provide the aggressive background for the 'family wars', both for the frequent 'war' between wife and husband, but also for the 'wars' between parents and children mentioned before.

What improves and heals

Condensed narrations of these dynamics can already be found in the early and earliest records and myths of mankind, such as the Epic of Gilgamesh, the Egyptian, Greek and Roman world of the gods, or in the biblical Genesis with its message of the alleged original sin plus 'expulsion from paradise'.

Some possible solutions to this 'trouble in Eden' have been presented in our novel 'The Pegasus Paradise'.
See *Bibliography*.

But this should not be the main focus here.

Rather, we'll concentrate on such methods of modern psychotherapy in this essay that are integrating aspects of depth-psychology with systemic and behavioural approaches in a way that appropriate developmental steps can be stimulated both for the *inner family* as well as for the *outer family* of the patient.

The round dance

The star of awareness shines now and never,
that's what your knee
under the table whispers to me
feeling connected and clever.

The coldest love now is glowing hate,
the double bass cheers us morning and late.

Doubts are arising as tall as they can -
but the luminous darkness heals woman and man.

And their Honey-Moon's music lights older folks smile
when even in winter a rice greens for a while.

From the Japanese Zen tradition

This story begins with a well-known and old **Zen master**, who is visited by a **man** with a question on his mind that keeps bothering him.

Therefore, the **man** approaches the master:
'People are often talking about heaven and hell - and I always wonder if those places exist at all?'

'Hm,' replies the **master**. And after a while:
'What profession do you practise?'

Now the **man** answers: 'I'm an officer in the army.'

Thereupon the **master**: 'Really? But that must have been a real straw head who appointed you an officer!
To my eyes, you look more like a butcher in a slaughter-house, I must say.'

Hearing this, the **officer** turned red with rage and began to draw his sword, shouting:
'How dare you! I'll cut you to pieces!'

At that moment, the **master** remarked:
'Look! Here you see the direct path to hell!'

Now the **officer** paused, smiled somewhat sheepishly and said:
'Please forgive me, I got carried away.'

Whereupon the **master** gave him a friendly look and explained:
'And now the path to heaven is visible as well.'

Advaita
Non-Duality

none
Love is none and Love is all,
Love is great and Love is small.
Fairy-wing and tiger tall:
Love is none and Love is all.

two
God is great and God is small,
God is none and God is all.
Fairy-wing and tiger tall:
God is great and God is small.

Imprinting in the family of origin

Dear reader, could it be that you are currently thinking about starting psychotherapy?
Or perhaps of becoming a therapist yourself?
In that case, you will find some useful reports and tools in this text, developed in the every night and everyday life of integrative psychotherapy.

All well and good, you may say - but what about that strange sentence on the front and back of this essay?

What is that supposed to mean?

'Dearest Mom, I know it's not new,
but to you I'll stay forever true!'
And:
'Dearest Dad, I know it's not new,
but to you I'll stay forever true!'

But who wants that now?

Core-sentences of child loyalty in conflict families
It is usually the children, who experience their parents in grief, conflict and suffering, who seem to 'want that'.

Because those children are mostly trying to support the desperate mother or discouraged father by being loyal and close to them so the family can remain stable.

Yet, it is this often far too 'unconditional loyalty' of the child towards a frustrated and needy parent that way too frequently leaves very restrictive or even dogmatic 'Sentences of Creed' in the child's psyche.

'Sentences of Creed' such as:
'This here is a TV-jungle camp with a level nine survival training - even if they pretend to be *Your Family!'*

'We show mutual closeness and affection by arguing with and shouting at each other, often very intensely and with a loud voice.'
'We show mutual closeness and affection by avoiding each other and keeping very quiet, sometimes for days or weeks on end.'

'About our bodies, sex, puberty and intimacy, we either keep quiet - or we don't talk about them - or we don't talk about them at all!'
'Feelings and understanding are not so important.
A sharp mind and rational intelligence are much more desirable.'

'If their Mom or Dad is doing so badly, the child has to help - but nobody must know about this special help and loyalty.'
'If it serves to stop its parents from constantly arguing or maybe splitting up, the child must even go further in its 'parent loyalty', for example by physically falling ill or by presenting mental problems.'

Restrictive effects later in life
And a 'Sentence of Creed' during adulthood:
'To the *Unconscient,* a functional and happy relationship in the present appears as a threat to the primary 'parent loyalty', which sometimes can trigger disturbances in the current partnership.'

Where a child's Basic Trust can unfold
Of course, there are also families with a more open and loving attitude, in which children are allowed to learn better 'Rules of Life'.
One example of a helpful variation will suffice here:

'My parents are friendly and close with each other and I can feel that they love me.
Like this, I'm allowed to be the way I am.'

But people with this kind of attitude or **Basic Trust** are only rarely asking for therapy.
Instead, it is usually people with a rather stressful and challenging situation in their lives who are appearing in therapy - and they are often limited by several of those 'Sentences of Creed' mentioned above, including early 'parent loyalty' imprinted in their personality.

Learning to be the therapist yourself
Let's assume for the moment that you - yes, that's right, you yourself! - are in the role of **therapist Cordula** now, who has been doing depth psychology-based psycho-therapy with her **patient Ernst** since a few months.

A patient called Ernst

But she had accepted this patient despite the fact that she had made an agreement with herself that she would only take patients into therapy in the future, who were in professional training, studying or had a steady job.
She had decided to implement this, when a number of experiences had shown her, how negatively a lacking job could influence any meaningful progress in therapy.

Work has priority
Therefore, she usually advised such patients to find a suitable job first, in order to ensure a more stable basis for a possible therapy.
Initially she had said something to that effect to patient Ernst, too. Ernst was in his early thirties, single and had completed his A-levels.
Next, he had found a flat for himself - but subsequently dropped out of two degree programmes.
He hailed from a simple middle-class family and had been born as the second of two children. In addition to his own odd jobs, he was still supported by his parents financially - if rather reluctantly by now.

An exception to the rule
But despite this partial 'nest sitter scenario' and the evident lack of work, Cordula - ignoring her own working rules - had taken this patient with his depressive-anxious symptoms into a short-term therapy, because she perceived in him a pressing suffering, good partial coping with life and a strong willingness to change himself.

And the introspective skills he showed, for example when working with his dreams, as well as his occasional shyly shimmering self-irony, had encouraged therapist Cordula that things would be different and better in this case - because Ernst was surely talented enough to find a good job and possibly also a fitting relationship?

Learned talented helplessness

But Cordula soon regretted that she had deviated from her own 'rule of acceptance'. In other words, from her commitment to the motto: First the material basis of existence must be a stable one, and only then in-depth therapeutic work with its emotional uncertainties can be embarked upon in a meaningful way.

Because now, her patient worked enthusiastically on all themes - whether early trauma caused by emotionally absent parents, whether later conflicts and break-ups in relationships. Also on dreams about his dropping out of his university studies. - But hardly anything happened in his real life for months.
No job applications and barley a few social contacts.

Taking care of the parents

Nevertheless, with her help, the patient was able to adopt a new perspective that enabled him to see that he was doing his estranged parents an important service with his 'talented helplessness'.

Cordula summarised it like this:

'So, Ernst, you really take care of your parents - with all the feelings you enable them to have, even if 'difficult feelings' as despair and anger are also involved!

Will they - your parents - be able to cope at all if you don't supply 'talented helplessness' to them any longer?'

Can parents tolerate the success of their children?

Can your parents really handle your professional success - or even a happy relationship? Who knows?

With this feedback, she reached Ernst in a more direct way than before - and in his dreams, the house of his family of origin, which had been the place of his child-hood and youth, was being renovated.

Who writes the job applications?

Things began moving a little, when the therapist, at the end of a rather uneventful session, had mentioned 'that unfortunately she couldn't write any job applications for the patient herself now, but as long as the therapy-sessions could take place as agreed and she was able to earn her money in peace, that would be fine . . .'

Only after this rather clear-cut paradoxical intervention by the therapist, Ernst, the patient, began researching and screening suitable job offers, followed by writing some initial job applications.

There even were some personal interviews.

But strangely enough, without any concrete results.

Now **Cordula** started having depressed feelings herself when she worked with this patient or even, when she just thought of him.

The case of patient Ernst in supervision
'Am I missing something here?,' she asked her experienced supervisor, to whom she was presenting the case.
'Because there are these strange dreams, in which Ernst dreamt that as a child he was looking for biscuits in the storeroom of his parents' flat when his father suddenly appeared. Then, depending on the dream, either a hat fell from the shelf onto his father's head - or the hat of the father fell from his head onto the floor.'

Working with dreams
Her **supervisor** then said with a friendly smile: 'It seems to me that you have already achieved quite a lot in a difficult situation - and these dreams are a present from your patient that speaks for itself.
How did you work with them?
Did the patient have any ideas connected with those dreams - or did you attempt a first interpretation?'

An early memory
Cordula: 'First I asked him about his own ideas about these dreams. He then recalled a 'biscuit tin can scene' from his childhood, when he was perhaps four years old, when he wanted to take some biscuits without having asked - not from the storeroom, however, but from a cupboard in the kitchen of the flat.

His Mom almost caught him, but he just managed to hide inside the cupboard.'

Supervisor: 'A clever little chap! But that's probably not the whole story, to venture a guess.
Or in other words, it could be a cover or interim memory that appears, before really traumatic experiences and memories can be contacted and processed.
But what about the storeroom?'

A meeting in the storeroom
Cordula: 'I realise that the actual themes of the patient are only partly visible in this biscuit memory. And a trial interpretation of the events related to his parents would certainly have been possible here.

Because when asked about the meaning of the store-room, the patient only remembered a 'rather queasy feeling' and a lump in his throat.

At that point I also pondered an interpretation.
However, because I have found with some patients that even very gentle trial interpretations can sometimes lead to defence and resistance, which can make further work very difficult, I finally decided to take a different approach in this case.'

The minus-plus dream
Supervisor: 'That sounds exciting.
What did your approach look like?'

Cordula: 'Quite simple: just like in real life.
Or in other words: ***The Minus-Plus Dream!***'

Supervisor: 'Huh?! Please excuse me - what exactly do you mean with this term: Plus-minus dream?'

The tragic variant of the dream
Cordula: 'Or maybe the other way around - anyhow, I told Ernst to take the *director's seat* in his own dreams, so he could develop two different 'dream film versions'.
First, a ***tragic version*** that shows what could happen in those dreams, in case conflict and escalation would be allowed to take place.
Ernst quickly arrived at a result: His father would realise that he wanted to nab some biscuits and perhaps even blame him for the falling hats.
In the worst case scenario, his Mom would also appear and join in the tirades.

A dream-like solution
Supervisor: 'Tough going! Bad; but close, the way it feels. Maybe something for later.
And was there another dream variant?'

Cordula: 'Yes, I asked him for *'a dream-like solution'*.
And in this ***Plus Dream*** that Ernst had imagined in the session, the hats all stayed on the shelf, while he and his Dad took some biscuits from the cupboard to share with his Mom and Ernst's brother in the kitchen.'

Supervisor: 'An overview or *synopsis of the two poles of the dream.* Great!
You have made good use of this opportunity to reinvent your therapeutic approach towards dreams.
Perhaps you can do something similar also in other areas of therapy?'

The patient in the therapist's dream
Cordula was grateful for this encouragement, but how exactly were things to proceed? Then she herself had a dream, in which her patient Ernst was packing a picnic basket for his parents, while he was wearing a hat!
Waking up, she was laughing about her dream, when she realised: 'It's his *childlike loyalty* to his parents.
That needs to be recognised and integrated.
Let's see how that might work . . .'

Finding the inner source
Therefore, one evening, after the last woman she had worked with had gone home, she took the time to think about possible steps for her future therapy-sessions with patient Ernst.
She sat down in her armchair in the therapy room and began to relax. As she had learnt in her teaching analysis and later in her meditation practice, she opened herself to her inner and wider awareness while she focused on the gently flowing waves of her breath.
At first she allowed herself to regenerate for some time, harboured safely in the middle of this calm and luminous darkness of her inner source.

Cordula's childhood

Then, some first images emerged on her inner screen, of her mostly happy childhood with her 'teacher-parents' and her siblings. She also saw scenes of her school days, accompanied by the sometimes difficult crises of her parents and her own distress at home.

Patient Ernst in the therapist's imagination

At this point, her patient Ernst is also slowly becoming visible and tangible.

At the same time, she is still seeing scenes from her medical studies, her further training as a specialist in general medicine and from her additional training as a psychotherapist in the background.

Suddenly she realises that *Sigmund Freud*, the founder of psychoanalysis and one of her great role models, appears in her inner image and then approaches her **patient Ernst**.

Freud is accompanied by *Lou Andreas Salomé*, who was trained by Freud in the early years of psychoanalysis and had later worked as a psychoanalyst herself.

A diagnosis by Dr Freud

Freud now explains to Mr **Ernst** his attachment to his parents in terms of a schizoid-oral neurotic structure, possibly with an Oedipal-psychosexual component.

'Yes, perhaps - but you can't tell him just like that!'

Cordula thinks immediately - and then sees how Freud is turning to her for a moment, giving her a kind smile and a wink of his eye.

A poem by Mrs Salomé

But before she can even begin to wonder about this, **Lou Andreas** is taking a step towards Mr **Ernst**, who is still looking at Sigmund Freud with a number of question marks in his eyebrows.

Lou touches Mr Ernst gently at his shoulder with her hand. Then she says softly:

'Sometimes'. And when Ernst is looking at her, she adds:
      'Who praises love, if just sometimes,
         has seen Vienna as it shines!'

Now she laughs at him, a bit mischievously, and then throws him a kiss, which he acknowledges with a rather wry smile.

'Well, well - look at that!,' **Cordula** is thinking during these inner images. But she remains relaxed and focused on her source. Then she witnesses, how *Anna Freud, Virginia Satir, Alfred Adler, Carl Gustav Jung* and *Mara Selvini-Palazzoli* - all professional role models of her - are beginning to talk to her patient Ernst.

A creative trance
But finally, her focus is shifting to a woman doctor, who used to be one of her training therapists and who, like her current supervisor, occasionally used techniques from **Fritz Perls'** *Gestalt Therapy*.

Cordula now sees an empty chair appearing opposite of Ernst, while her former teaching therapist is pointing at this *Empty Chair.*

The Empty Chair
'Aha, the Empty Chair then. Which perhaps means that he should communicate his loyalty directly to his mother or father. And he can imagine them on this Empty Chair, here, during the session.

But rational speech and interpretations have their limits - what should he say to his mother that confirms and relieves him in his loyalty to her - and at the same time invites real change into his life?

On this, she once again sees *Lou Andreas Salomé's* smile, who touches her lips with her index finger with a *'Shh!'*

A retro poem
'Maybe it should be something paradoxical,' **Cordula** thinks. - Perhaps a poem like the one from Lou before - only different again . . . yes, that could be it:

'Dearest Mom, I am still small,
that's why I'm yours for now and all!'

'Yes,' thinks Cordula, while she is emerging from her creative trance, 'that could work. -
And it's paradoxical for sure.
But first I'll discuss it in supervision next week.'

Yes she can!
Then she remembers: 'Hm - but I should probably try it out myself first, before I offer this paradoxical impulse to other people or patients. All right then.

With these thoughts in mind, Cordula gets up and goes to a chair at the side of the therapy room.
She then places this chair in the centre of the room opposite her armchair. Now she sits down again and looks at the empty chair in front of her.

A sentence for the mother
'Maybe I'll start with Mom, that's somewhat easier,' she thinks. Then she visualises her mother as best she can - the way she remembers her from her childhood.
And then she tries out the poem she had found earlier, first quietly and inwardly.
But then also saying it out loud:
'Dearest Mom, I am still small,
that's why I'm yours for now and all!'

Now she pauses for a moment, breathes and collects herself, and then says this sentence again from her center and with calm and strength in her voice.

'Well now,' she thinks, 'mostly there's lots of gratitude and trust towards her, apart from a few scenes when I was in puberty and we sometimes had minor disagreements about outfits, skirt length or make-up - oh-là-là!'

With some friendly words for her mother, Cordula now gets up and puts the empty chair back at the side of the room. Then she chooses another chair, which she places opposite herself.

Doubts and uncertainty
'Yes, this is better suited for Dad,' she thinks as she sits down again. Gradually, she is beginning to recognise the outlines of her father in the empty chair, while the 'small and all' phrase is jingling in her mind already.

But suddenly she feels uneasy and insecure. Now there is her great father, who always knew and accomplished everything - and she has nothing better to do than telling him this somehow childish phrase!
At this point, she realises how a mixture of sadness, anxiety and anger is beginning to rise up inside of her.
'Amazing!,' thinks Cordula, 'and I haven't even said anything yet.' And then: 'But where these difficult feelings are, there is often a chance for further personal development, as the saying goes.

And a sentence for the father
So let's get on with it!
And although she feels a little chilly and uneasy, she says the sentence:
'Dearest Dad, I am still small
therefore I'm yours for now and all!'
loud and clear now, right in the direction of the image of her father.

Even as she is still saying this sentence, she is surprised to feel tears running down her face.

Crisis years of the parents

Then she remembers: 'Oh my goodness! The crisis years - it seems I managed to forget about those years almost completely.'

She was around seven to ten years old at the time, and it was the phase of those 'secret meetings' with her older sister and younger brother, in order to find solutions for their parents.

Encouraging the father

Now she sees some scenes, in which her sad father was rather dejected and she tried to cheer him up by giving him a hug.

Sometimes, when her father was in a particularly low mood, she would even run to her hiding place with the 'iron reserve candy stash' and bring him one or two of her drops, perhaps with the words:

'Life soon can taste sweet again as well, Dad!,' which - at least occasionally - seemed to help him.

Parents in limbo

Then she sometimes mustered the courage to ask him a direct question:

'Tell me Dad, do you and Mom still love each other?'

And **Cordula** sees how her father is smiling at her, in that scene back then, while he is tilting his head slightly.

For a moment, then as now, she is holding her breath.

After a while, she hears her **father** say: 'You know, that's exactly what we're trying to find out right now.

And we definitely love you and each other.

But it's all gotten so much - and with all this routine and responsibility, we haven't really found enough time for each other.

So now we need a new beginning, and we agree on that, which is a start!'

'New beginning, new beginning, new beginning,' it echoes inside of **Cordula**.

At the same time, her **father** starts talking again - to her as a child, back then.

A new start for the family

Father: 'And maybe you children could support us a little in this - like helping with the housework from time to time, or tidying up your rooms - and maybe even going to bed voluntarily, now and then, things like that, what do you think?'

'That's definitely possible,' **she sees herself** answer with childlike enthusiasm, 'the others will definitely agree, if I talk to them; oh, well, and you and Mom too, of course!'

'That would be great,' her **father** replies, 'but one thing is clear, the task of clarifying and hopefully healing our relationship lies with your Mom and me - with **Barbara** and me, that is. But thank you for your questions and your help,' she still hears her **father Joseph** add.

Transformative years with couples therapy
'My goodness, I had completely forgotten about that - maybe even repressed it! - How stressful and close that was for Babs and Jo back then!
Rarely were we kids as well-behaved and co-operative as during those *'transformer years'*, as Dad sometimes used to call them later on.'

Finally, their parents had several sessions with a skilled couple's therapist.
There they learnt or re-learnt how to stop endless arguments elegantly - and how to share a hug, a compliment or a kiss instead, which already had a very positive effect on their parents' mood.

Parents' weekends
The therapist's most important intervention, however, was her recommendation to plan a parents' weekend every month of the year, with nanny, grandma or aunt supervision for the children.

And although she and her siblings initially were not very enthusiastic about the idea of parent-free weekends, the children later had to admit that it was not least these relatively rare, two-day 'vacations' as a couple that had brought Babs and Jo, their parents, much closer together again.
Just in time for them as a couple. And exactly in time for Cordula's younger brother, who was invited into the family's nest on one of these couple weekends.

Surprise offspring

At the time, she and her siblings were worried that the new baby - and therefore four children in total - would be too much of a burden for their parents.

'But things turned out very differently,' **Cordula** remembers now, wiping the remaining tears from her eyes.

'Little **Jonas** became the sunshine of the family - and everyone continued to blossom and thrive!

This was also possible, because the occasional grandma, uncle or nanny days were retained by the parents in a baby-adapted form.

And I had 'forgotten' most of it! So this sentence seems to be quite useful after all, as far as I can tell.

A St Martin's procession

But now home to **Daniel** and our children!

It's a good thing the lights are on here in the city,' thinks **Cordula**, wrapped up warmly as she cycles with her bike through the early winter cold and darkness.

On the way, she suddenly hears:

'Thought about by everyone
bringing the light by all was done.
Oh, what joy, oh, what fun!'*

She thinks:

'Evidently a St Martin's procession of schoolchildren, and that here in Munich.

But their teacher seems to be from the Rhineland, according to her accent!'

*'Thought of by every girl and boy
all brought their light, now ain't that coy.
Oh, what fun, oh, what joy!'

She soon reaches the aged but well-kept building in one of the quieter and greener neighbourhoods of the city, where she is living with her patch-work family.
She is happy to see them all again.

Daniel, her boyfriend and fiancé, then **Pierre** - her newly grown-up son from her brief relationship with **Serge** during her semester abroad in Paris - and finally **Luna**, Daniel's and her daughter, who is now attending kindergarten since some time.

Cordula and Daniel's patchwork family
After Cordula has taken off her winter clothes, she is hugged by everyone, with Luna not wanting to let go of her leg.
'It's great you're here now!,'
says **Daniel**, holding Cordula in his arms.
'But what happened? Usually, you're home earlier.'

'That's right. Oh dear!,' **Cordula** replies as she looks at her watch. 'It was kind of an emergency, a patient, for whom I wanted to develop a different treatment format. That's why I still went into a creative trance after the sessions - and I must have forgotten about time in the process.
I'm so sorry! Please excuse me!'

Pierre: *'Maman, Maman,* your excuses are always getting - *comment dit on?* - how do you say? - *plus éxotiques!* More and more exotic! *Admirable!* Remarkable!'

After this tender and bilingual admonition, Pierre gives her a kiss on the cheek before throwing on his jacket and scarf with the cryptic remark:
'Student meeting!'

'I thought we were having dinner together now,' **Cordula** replies.
'Yes, that's what we thought too,' adds **Luna**, who is holding on to Cordula's leg like a little monkey.
'But only for a while - then it just smelled too good . . .
And you're lucky that Daniel has saved everything for you!,' she says, while she's running ahead to the table.

'Au revoir,' **Pierre** says goodbye now to everyone, giving them all a quick hug.
'Bonne chance! - Good luck!,' says **Cordula**, 'and return for a visit sometime.'
Then, together with Daniel and Luna, she walks over to the dining table in their spacious kitchen.

Dinner together
Daniel places a plate of steaming, vegetarian-biodynamic pasta with tomato sauce and Parmesan cheese on Cordula's plate, followed by a mixed salad with olives and goat's cheese, a cup of hot herbal tea and a glass of still water.

'What a service! You're really pampering me,' **Cordula** comments with a grateful smile as she sits down in front of the inviting food.

Daniel: 'You've had a rather long day - and I only had the children in the afternoon.
Now eat and regenerate in peace for a while. And if you like, you can tell me about your new concept later on.'
At this point, little **Luna** starts to squawk a little, until **Daniel** remembers: 'Oh yes! I almost forgot - Luna learnt a little English grace for the kids at the kindergarten today that she really wanted to teach you.
Isn't that right, Luna?'

An English grace from kindergarten
'Oh yes,' says **Luna**, and: 'Now listen!'
Then she stands up and declaims almost fluently:
'Rubba dub-dub,
Thanks for the grub!
Yeah Lord!'
And while Cordula is still blinking several times, Luna is explaining with a knowing smile:
'Our teacher in kindergarten said, the meaning is something like this in German - wait a minute, yes now:
'Dank Dir, oh Herr, für diesen Brei,
denn der macht uns im Bäuchlein frei!'   In English:
'Thank you, oh Lord, for this good food,
for it brings to our tummies a happy mood!'

'Great!,' says **Cordula**, impressed by Luna's performance, while she continues to tuck into her pasta and salad.
Then she adds:
'A beautiful poem - both in English and German.
Thank you for memorising it!'

Luna is delighted. But then she demands:
'And now all together, even if you've started already!'

The magic word
But soon after they've done *'Rubba dub-dub'* together,
little **Luna** is suddenly getting very tired, as she usually
does around this time early in the evening.
Therefore she asks her father:
'Daddy, will you still tell me a story before bedtime?'

To which **Daniel** replies:
'And what's the magic word?'

And in tune with the rules of this timeless game, **Luna**
responds with a sleepy *'Pleeeeazze!'*

'All right,' says **Daniel**, 'then I'll put you to bed now.'
And towards Cordula:
'I'll be back in a minute and we can talk.'

And while she enjoys the rest of her meal, she hears
Daniel and Luna's voices from the children's room until
Daniel begins to tell the story of a princess called Sleeping Beauty, which Luna - along with Rumpelstiltskin -
particularly loves.

Sheep, twigs and dreams
But then **Daniel** reappears and explains:
'She still wants us to sing *'Sleep, Baby sleep!'* for her, and
both of us together.'

Cordula rolls her eyes a bit, but then agrees.
And a few sheep, Moms and Dads, small twigs and some dream showers later, Luna has actually fallen asleep.
Now Cordula and Daniel are sitting down together in the kitchen again.

Daniel had studied psychology and was a healing practitioner. He had then trained as a behavioural therapist and now worked in an *MVZ,* a *medical care centre* that had specialised in the fields of psychiatry, psychotherapy and psychosomatics.

The two had first met during the *Lindau Psychotherapy Weeks* and later became a couple.
By now, they were planning their wedding - 'before we turn forty!' - also because of Luna.

A new tool for later use
'So,' asks **Daniel**, 'does it fit for you now, to talk about what you've found at the practice, during your creative imagination?'

'Sure,' answers **Cordula**, 'it's a kind of paradoxical poem that might help some patients to contact their frequent, childlike and usually quite unconditional loyalty to their parents.

And further, to recognise and appreciate their loyalty as a service both to their parents and their family.

This contributes to a benevolent integration and transformation of those rather disturbing and pathological infantile tendencies towards parent-oriented loyalty.
Which often allows for new possibilities and degrees of freedom in their present relationship.
Oh, speaking of the present: The food was great, thank you very much!'

'You're welcome!,' says **Daniel**.
And: 'Wow, now I'm really interested in that new rhyme of yours, after that special announcement!'

'I understand that very well,' replies **Cordula**, 'and of course, you'll be the first person, whom I'm going tell this sentence.
But it's all so very fresh still - and I'd like to sleep on it for at least a night or two before I talk about it any further. Maybe at the weekend?
But tell me, how was your day? You're in a good mood, as almost always, but at the same time you seem a bit worn - hopefully not because of the children?'

Daniel: 'No, no, the kids were great.
And that's a good thing about talking at the weekend - maybe your dreams will give you some further input for your new concept.

Daniel's day at the practice
Apart from that, you're right; my morning at the medical care center was pretty special!

I almost have to assume that our head of psychiatry is trying to give me a hard time.'

Cordula: 'What makes you think that, I thought you got on quite well together?'

Daniel: 'So far, yes. But this morning he slapped me with three difficult patients at once.
That smells like a system!'

Cordula: 'Poor you! But take it easy - maybe *'Dr House'*, as you sometimes call him, just wants to test you and see what skills you got?'

Thinking, Humming and Being

Cogito, ergo sum.   *To think is to be.* *
René Descartes

Hum, ergo sum.   *To hum is to be.* *
Maya the Bee

*Literal translation: *I think, therefore I am.*
And: *I hum, therefore I am.*

Difficult patients: Cynthia, Patrizia and Bernd

Patient Cynthia

'Ha!' **Daniel** replies to her. 'The first patient is in her mid-twenties, would look good if she didn't have anorexia, has problems with her job as a 'management consultant' at an IT service provider and therefore wants to quit. - Yes, and then a relationship broke up six months ago.

And she has quite acute suicidal thoughts, with a most likely appellative suicide attempt in her case history.'

Cordula: 'My goodness!
But I've also had similar patients before.

Now, before we talk about this patient any further, who were the others?'

Daniel: 'Not as dramatic as with **Cynthia**, as I'm calling this first patient, but also stranger than usual.

The second was a young man in his thirties, whom we'll call **Bernd** here. This patient is talking about his work in marketing as well as his marriage in very vague ways:

'Does our product really fit one of the possible markets?'
Or: 'My wife and I have such different parenting styles, how can this make sense for the children?!'
At the same time, I can't feel any particularly pronounced suffering pressure.'

Cordula: 'Quite different from Cynthia's case!
And patient number three?'

Daniel twists his face and raises his eyebrows a little:
'That was a woman in her mid-forties, whom I'll call
Patrizia here, and who greeted me with such a torrent
of words, a veritable *logorrhoea*, so I had real trouble to
even ask a single question myself.
Now that her three children are grown up, she is working again - without having to - as an administrative
manager in an office.
Her husband is an expert in genetic research, which has
recently given him even more responsibility, resulting in
less time for his family.
When she mentions the differences with her husband,
this woman jumps up from her seat several times and
then begins shouting her themes at me - from a distance
of hardly thirty centimetres.'

Cordula: 'What nerve! And you - how did you react?'

Daniel: 'After I'd gotten over the initial shock, I pulled
out my *'just in case'* Corona mask and shouted, waving
the mask:
Aerosols! That's far too close for me!
Please sit down again!'

Cordula: 'And did she?'

Daniel: 'Eventually yes, after three or four attempts.'

Cordula: 'Oh dear. But can you work with this woman?'

Daniel: 'Wait and see.
We've made another appointment. And maybe I should see her husband at some point, also.'

Cordula: 'Well, to see her partner and hear what he has to say is certainly useful as a complementary perspective. But I still have this first patient Cynthia in my head. How did it go with her?'

Patient Cynthia continued
Daniel: 'According to the protocol for such acutely vulnerable patients - presumably similar to yours, in your group practice, where you surely also have a protocol for such cases?'
Cordula nods and Daniel continues: 'First of all, I offered Cynthia another appointment to clarify the possible options and to find out more about her family of origin.
As usual, I also suggested a contract that stated that she contacts me, the MVZ or a clinic before she starts any suicide preparations.'

Cordula: 'Was she able to accept this contract like that?'

Daniel: 'At first she hesitated briefly, but then we shook hands on it - and she gave me a smile, as it seemed, but with a rather hard look. Well then. And the patient was given an appointment with our psychiatrist immediately, also according to protocol.

Before that, I had already told Cynthia about the option of a **Ketamine® therapy** *for acute depression.*
She had even heard of this method, but was 'against all medication.'
Our **Dr Müller** then discussed this topic with her in more detail:
Possible anti-depressants to help in bridging the severe depression; or a therapy trial with a *Ketamine® nasal spray;* possibly plus a therapy trial with *Ketamine® infusions,* lasting about 45 minutes, with therapeutic support.

No medication!
And finally, the possibility of a voluntary admission to a psychiatric clinic, to have the acute depression treated there.
Cynthia, however, rejected all of these offers, declaring that she hoped to cope better with her mood-swings with the help of the therapy sessions.'

Cordula: 'A lot of trust in the strong healing power of the therapist!
And how are you feeling with all of that?'

Daniel: 'Overburdened, of course!
How is that ever supposed to work?'

Cordula: 'Maybe first by expanding your breathing again, here, to your belly and also there, into your heart area?,' she asks, while she's gently stroking him there.

'And then: Who is responsible for the life of this young woman now, who has a lot of suffering in her life, but is also very self-assured in her decisions?'

Daniel: 'She herself, of course.
But still, this situation was not an easy one for me.'

A Double Bind in therapy
Cordula: 'This woman is even giving me mixed feelings, just from hearing your report!

This pronounced double-sided aspect of her, similar to **Gregory Bateson's** *Double Bind.*
I've got some doubts, if that can ever work, just with psychotherapy alone?'

Daniel: 'And so do I. Sure, I could have sent her on her way with a clear conscience because of that. With those recommendations by Dr Müller, our psychiatrist. But firstly, the patient definitely didn't want any medication.

Cancelled therapies in the past
And then there was something else still:
She mentioned that in the past she had started three therapies already, but all of her therapists had stopped them after twenty or thirty hours because they couldn't help her any further, as they said.'

Cordula: 'Well. What a treasure!
A suicidal therapist killer! Dear - how did you continue?'

Inviting options for the next year

Daniel: 'I needed a moment to sort things out.
And further information about Cynthia. Therefore I had her draw a picture. I gave her a large drawing pad with coloured wax crayons and asked her to sketch two to four situations that she wanted to invite into her life during the next year.

Then she painted and I had time to take notes, calm my mind and find first ideas for a suitable plan.

Scenes from the future

In the meantime, Cynthia had drawn three tiny scenes with the coloured crayons, all the way at the bottom left of the page:

First, a holiday landscape with a beach, sun loungers and shade-giving palm trees; next a group of friends hiking in the mountains and then partying at a table later on; and finally a desk with a PC in a room with a view towards nature, which she briefly commented with the words: 'My new job!'

Suddenly, she had the brief impulse to cross everything out and paint it over in black, but I managed to distract her from that by appreciating her pictures as meaningful and also, by asking her about a possible fourth scene, for example with her best woman friend?

Then I removed the picture from the pad, photographed it for documentation and gave the original to her.'

Cordula: 'Sure, but then what? Good idea with that picture - but what agreement did you make? Did you offer her ongoing therapy? Be careful! Be very careful!'

Daniel: 'No, I didn't. Instead, I made it clear to her how difficult her form of work offer was for me, if she rejected all the other recommendations, which is why she should consider them again and especially the option of *Ketamine® nasal spray*.

Otherwise, as I'd mentioned earlier, I only gave her one further consultation appointment in two weeks - but no firm commitment to ongoing treatment for the moment, as she would have wanted.'

Cordula: 'Wow. I'm not sure if I could work with this patient . . . but at least she has painted those pictures.'

Daniel: 'Exactly. And this next appointment will give her the security of getting another session, where she can consider and discuss everything in peace with me.'

Happy Hour for the therapists
When they have finished their exchange, Cordula and Daniel call it a day.

After a shower together, they listen to some quiet music and meditate for a while before embarking on the profoundest and all-renewing meditation of deep sleep.

Later in this text, we'll return to Cynthia and to Daniel's other two patients. That will be in the section:
'Difficult Patients Part II'.

The 'small and all' sentence in a test phase
On the weekend after this conversation, **Cordula** explained her new-found sentence to Daniel while they were taking a walk:
'Dearest Mom, I am still small,
that's why I'm yours for now and all!'
Or:
'Dearest Dad, I am still small,
that's why I'm yours for now and all!'

'Sounds rather trivial, I know,' **Cordula** admitted. 'But if you really want to find out what this paradoxical rhyme can do, it's best to find a quiet time, where you try it out for yourself,' she explained.
Daniel: 'This compact verse definitely is a direct invitation into the early years of childhood,' he said, blinking several times.
'But I'd rather do that just like you, in a peaceful setting - and while making use of the *Empty Chair.'*
And in supervision
When **Cordula** had her next supervision a while later, she told the professor about her new-found sentence:
'Dearest Mom, I am still small,
that's why I'm yours for now and all!,'
she explained, but at first she saw little response in his elder and composed face.

But suddenly his expression came alive - sad, but also cheerful and angry features alternated now, while his eyes were half closed.

A moment later, however, they were all open again and looked straight at her.

'Well, ain't that's something!,' her **supervisor** remarked, while sporting an otherwise rarely shown maximum of emotions.

'But there is - it's good, you know - and it might have a useful potential - but isn't there something missing still? And when and with whom is it safe to use this tool?'

Cordula: 'I've been thinking about that too, since I had this new experience with this verse and the *Empty Chair* - yes, this new insight . . . sure, that could be it!

The 'true and new' version
What do you think of this variation?'
Then Cordula declaims the rhyme:

'Dearest Mom, I know it's not new,
but to you I'll stay forever true!'
And:
'Dearest Dad, I know it's not new,
but to you I'll stay forever true!'

After a while, her **supervisor** comments with the faintest hint of a smile: 'Absolutely. Oh yes.

And you obviously took my advice the other day right to heart, to possibly find new avenues in your therapeutic approach with your patient Ernst.

And the result is - yes, remarkable at least.
But kindly be very careful with this so newly discovered instrument.
The reactions of the patients to this verse could be very unpredictable - and not only those of the patients!'

Methodological and safety questions
'How do you mean that?,' **Cordula** asked.
Supervisor: 'Can't you see that yourself? There could be some colleagues who would be inclined to take a critical stance towards such an approach in therapy.
In any case, we should talk further about it, before you use this phrase with other people besides your patient Ernst.'
Cordula: 'Yes, that's fine with me, too; all of this is quite new territory.
Even though similar methods exist already, for example by **Virginia Satir, Mara Selvini-Palazzoli, Bert Hellinger** or **Milton Erickson,** which we've already talked about.
Above all, however, my own experiences with this therapeutic verse motivate me to use it in a careful way when it fits the situation of the patient.'

Later Cordula said goodbye to a somewhat thoughtful **'Dr Jones'**, as she inwardly had named her supervisor - because he was, among other role-models, a real 'Freud-fan', just like **Dr Ernest Jones**, Freud's biographer from the very origins of psychoanalysis.
Her supervisor also gave her another appointment in the near future for the next supervision session.

Patient Ernst continued
But how did things go on with Cordula's patient Ernst?
When he was once again complaining at length about his lack of motivation for any job research or for writing job applications during a session, **Cordula** now suggested a switch in the level of the exchange, with the help of the first version of the sentence she had found.

She explained to him how he could use the *Empty Chair* method and how to combine it with the 'small and all' sentence.

As **Ernst** felt more emotional closeness to his mother, **Cordula** instructed him to say the sentence to her.
'What if I don't want to do that?,' **Ernst** asked.
Cordula: 'You don't have to do anything, Ernst.
The sentence also works in silence - just as you like. But saying it loud to your mother here could help a lot in integrating your childlike loyalty towards her, those old ties that you've encountered several times in our work already. And integrating them better may give you more freedom and new options in the ways you behave and how you experience the present.'

Small and all
After a short pause, **Ernst** replies with a Sphinx-like face: 'All right then.'
Now he looks directly at the empty chair in front of him and then takes a deeper breath:
'Dearest Mom, I am still small,
therefore I'm yours for now and all.'
'What kind of bull . . . I mean nonsense is that?!,'
he exclaims, not a second later.

Cordula: 'Yes, that's a very paradoxical sentence, you're right - but that's the only way it can work in a healing way. Try it again, letting go of any judgement, but with a collected and composed attitude - if you want to do that.'

And **Ernst** repeats the sentence, a little slower now - and his voice sounds calmer and fuller.

Construction site in the supermarket
'Just like that,' **Cordula** confirms his concentrated effort.

Now **Ernst** is suddenly remembering a long-forgotten situation from when he was about four or five years old.
Together with his rather rational and absent-minded mother, he had been to the supermarket, where he got lost in the pet department.
And his mother, in her own shopping list trance, had left without him.

When nobody looked out for him, he had built himself a little house, making use of the pet food boxes on the shelf. And in this makeshift hut he was later found by a shop assistant.
As soon as he was discovered, the search was on for his mother, both in the shop and also in the parking area.
There she was found, when she had just returned in her car, because she, while 'on the road again', had finally noticed Ernst's absence.

Ernst: 'She could at least have apologised for forgetting me there.
But she just yelled at me.'

'Maybe you've experienced your Mother in a rather confused and desperate state back then?,' **Cordula** asks.

True and new
To this **Ernst** is nodding at first.
But then hangs his head a little.
'That's the moment to give it a chance!,' **Cordula** thinks.
Then she explains the second version of her new found sentence to patient Ernst:

'Dearest Mom, I know it's not new,
but to you I'll stay forever true!'

When **Ernst** hears this sentence for the first time, he suddenly looks straight at her - and with that trace of a mischievous smile on his changed face.
A smile that she had only seen once on him before.

An English motto for life
It was in one of the first sessions that she had asked Ernst for a motto or slogan for his life.
'I don't really have one . . .,' he had begun at the time.
'Except - ,' and then that half 'in spite of everything' smile, 'except for that English two-liner that you might know already?'
'What's that now?,' **Cordula** had asked him at the time.

To which **Ernst** replied:
'I am nobody.
Nobody is perfect.'
And once again that boyish smile, so very different from his usual face.
That had been the moment, when Cordula decided to take Ernst into therapy, even though he met her admission criteria only in part.

Cordula: 'You're smiling like you did back then, in one of the first sessions. Would you like to try out this 'true and new' sentence for yourself?'

Understanding a child's loyalty
'Yes,' says **Ernst**, 'I can go along with that form somewhat better - and I should certainly be faithful to my Mom, shouldn't I?'

Cordula: 'Of course. That's what this work is all about, that we recognise and appreciate those loyalties from childhood, so you can give your mother and father the fitting place of honour in your heart.
Even if the first place in your heart may later belong to a partner.
But for now, you can simply try out this variant of the sentence, if you want', she says, pointing to the empty chair.

When **Ernst** has also said this 'new and true' sentence to his Mom, he suddenly starts chuckling quietly.

'What's happening to you now?,' asks **Cordula**.

The graduation party

And **Ernst** replies: 'I just remembered my A-levels, when I was a bit tipsy at a graduation party - and was suddenly kissed by a girl.'

Cordula: 'That sounds interesting. So apart from your loyalty to your mother, there's obviously room for new encounters, even back then, during your A-levels.'

Ernst: 'Maybe. But unfortunately, there was no chance for us, because of her boyfriend.

And all my other attempts . . .,' he ends.

Cordula: 'So far that may have been the case, but what happened at the graduation party remains anyway.

And now you've let this 'new and true' sentence into your life that recognises and integrates your loyalty to your parents.

Continue with it in peace and try it out in a quiet setting, so you can discover how it might benefit you.'

Some time after this session, Ernst now began to tackle the job searches and writing of applications he had been putting off due to his lack of motivation previously.

And only a short time later, he was able to inform his surprised and grateful therapist about a job he had found in a warehouse, where he managed the storage area at a small industrial company.

'It's really not my dream job,' **Ernst** had commented on the otherwise good news of finally getting work.

Cordula: 'But you've found a job, you've been working there for a few weeks now and you get on quite well with your colleagues - and you did that despite these rather pronounced ambivalences about beginning anything at all. Congratulations!'

When the approved therapy contingent of fifty hours of depth psychology based therapy, usually in intervals of two to three weeks, was slowly drawing to an end, Ernst had made some further changes in his professional development.

This option was possible now, when he had successfully completed advanced qualifications in computer- and internet-technology.
This had brought him a much better job offer with more personal responsibility at a heat pump company.

The timing for a pause in therapy
There had even been a date at some point - with a woman 'who didn't really fit with me that well,' as **Ernst** himself had admitted.
But he wanted to continue his therapy with Cordula.

Cordula answered:
'First of all, thank you for your trust in our work, Ernst. And yes, we could apply for some more hours. But when we consider everything you've achieved during this time of our cooperation, I think we should at least make room for a pause at the moment.'

And as Ernst looked a bit disappointed at her, she still added:
'And in case of emergency, you could contact me.

But there's another reason for our planning a pause in therapy now.
Because you've meanwhile created such a stable basis for yourself that you could perhaps try to find, chart and set your own future course in life at this point.

Because alone often doesn't mean lonely only - it can also mean 'all at one' - or in connection with everything. As in this poem:

alone

Be as you are
to the whole take a stance.

And when as a couple
music beckons to dance:

Then be as you are
see the whole at a glance.

Or in other words,' she adds - in response to a some-what confused expression on Ernst's face - 'according to my experience, people, including patients, usually don't like it so much when they feel observed while they are in the process of falling in love.

In this case, further therapy itself can become a real obstacle or even a dead end road - and we can prevent this cul-de-sac by planning a pause in therapy, as we're doing now.

Additionally, I've got some literature recommendations for you, which you can use to continue working on your-self whenever that fits for you.'

See *Bibliography*.

A greeting card

Some time later, Cordula received a greeting card from a beautiful holiday destination.

It said:

'Thank you for the creative pause in therapy.'

And underneath it stated:

Ernst

Time as an entity
is the serenity
of all eternity.

'Who would ever have guessed that?,' **Cordula** asked herself quietly, while she placed the card in Mr Ernst's patient file.

With that, we move on from Cordula and her patient Ernst to the three patients whom Daniel had recently mentioned in the chapter 'Difficult Patients Part I'.

Difficult Patients Part II

Looking back, **Daniel** summarised the development in those three therapies as follows:

Patient Patrizia

'Let's start with **Patrizia**, the anxious-depressed patient with panic attacks for 'trivial reasons', who is the woman with the loud and empathy-lacking behaviour in the first session, which caused me to ask her several times to kindly sit down again.

After seeing her together with her husband, **Ulrich**, and then also talking to him in an individual session, I was gradually beginning to understand her situation a little better.

During these sessions and in the further work with Patrizia, it became clear that the couple - she in her mid-forties, he in his late forties - had three children, who all had left their parents' house now, some already having their own families.

Ulrich had then buried himself even more in his work in genetic research.

Shortly after the last child moved out, Ulrich suffered a sudden loss of hearing.

Although he was treated immediately with infusions in the hospital, he still needed a hearing aid from then on.

And he had found out quickly, how he could keep the sometimes 'annoying environment' at a quiet distance with the help of his tiny volume control.

Learned infringement

Patrizia, his wife, had adapted to this with her apparent lack of distance by now, as she was shouting into his ear from close quarters.

And he also had moderate **AD(H)S**, an **A**ttention **D**eficit (**H**yperactivity) **S**yndrome, which Ulrich had shown as a child and teenager already. It occasionally posed some problems for his team at work and for his wife at home.

Everyone constantly had to clean up after him, 'because he's the great scientist! But there's hardly any time left for us now - as it seems, he can't hear me at all with this strange new hearing device,' commented **Patrizia**, who was milling thoughts of separating already.

An AD(H)S therapy trial

But then **Daniel** showed the couple some simple but trust-building communication exercises, in which they both cooperated and made closer emotional contact again. Finally, Daniel was able to motivate Ulrich to get a prescription, so he could try a therapy for his AD(H)S with low-dose *Methylphenidate*, sustained-release form.

Patrizia reported: 'And then I got this call from **Julia**, his 'right-hand woman', the junior professor at the institute, with whom I have been friends for a long time.'

So **Julia** asked me: 'What have you done to him?

Suddenly he's almost like a normal person - we even laughed together!

Laughing with Ulrich - are you having your fifth spring or something?'

Patrizia kept her secret, of course, but at the same time told Julia that her guess was 'pretty close', which is why the team at the institute would unusually have to make do without Ulrich the next weekend, as she would be spending it with him in a nice hut in the mountains with no internet connections.

A while later, Daniel agreed with Patrizia and Ulrich to end therapy.
They had now turned into a different and more relaxed couple, as he wrote in the last notes he made.

Patient Bernd
Daniel: 'Initially, I only had a vague impression of that other candidate on that memorable day, who is called **Bernd** here. This patient was in his early thirties, married and had three smaller children.

Bernd was a qualified engineer in a good position, but he complained about a lack of sleep, appetite and motivation and about tensions in his marriage.'
Nevertheless, Daniel found it difficult to identify any clearly pressing suffering in Bernd, as most areas of his life appeared to be well resolved.

This was also because the patient had already managed to quit his somewhat insecure job at a smaller, very experimental IT company during the counselling sessions with Daniel, when he had signed a better contract with a larger enterprise.

But despite this professional success, he was further plagued by severe mood swings, by nightmares with dangerous pursuers and by frequent arguments with his wife, **Uta**.

An arguing couple

Bernd said: 'But things are just getting better, the little one is now going to kindergarten, the middle one, too and the older one is at school already. This enabled Uta to start working at that PR agency again, part-time, where she shares the management with a colleague.

And she enjoys being creative in her job again. And now that new job for me, so everything is better than ever, actually. But we argue about the children's education, about organising our free time - and about the cleaning schedule - even things have been thrown already!'

Skills for de-escalation

Daniel showed Bernd some simple 'coping skills' or behavioural strategies that he could use to avoid escalating arguments - such as leaving the room, drinking a glass of cool water or going for a walk.

Daniel also offered to see Bernd and Uta together in a session to better understand their situation, as a couple and as a family.

During this session, it suddenly became clear that **Uta** was on the verge of ending the relationship, so she could later file for a divorce.

As a child, Uta herself had experienced how her father had left the family, something she still had dark dreams about from time to time.

Old bills
Daniel explained these dynamics to her, saying:
'You may want to punish your father - but the damage would be done to yourself, your husband Bernd, who loves you very much despite those constant arguments - and above all, to your three young children, whom you would transfer into a patchwork family.
And when they reach puberty at the latest, your children will ask you: 'Why did you do that to us?'

Constructive controversial discussion
Finally, Daniel showed the couple the exercise:
'Constructive controversial discussion with one leg up', a variation based on **Milton Erickson**, in which both partners of the arguing couple each put one leg up during the exchange, for example on a chair, stool or sofa, and continue their discussion in this position.

A really good week
A while after this session with the couple, Bernd came back to Daniel for a one-to-one session.
Bernd, who seemed cool or depressed most of the time, had already given Daniel an almost conspiratory smile when he greeted him.
Then he talked about 'a really good week' that he and Uta had shared - including a lovely and for both orgiastic erotic night.

Daniel was surprised and grateful at once to see this sudden improvement for the couple.

He supported Bernd and Uta in their flexibility and fore-sight, which would certainly also turn out to be a benefit for their children.

Then Bernd still drew a picture in that session, in which he detailed, among other things, future trips and activities as a couple and with the family, making use of a drawing pad and coloured wax crayons.

Opposing forces

But when the patient came to the *MVZ* or *medical care center* for his next appointment, he seemed even darker and more depressed to Daniel than in the first hours of therapy.

As soon as he was in the therapy room **Bernd** burst out: 'Now she's breaking up with me after all - and this time it's definite!,' while he broke into tears.

Just a few days after that wonderful night of love, **Uta** had told him that 'this was all well and good, but she still had to end their relationship,' without giving any specific reasons that Bernd had asked for.

Daniel: 'But how can she go on and separate, just in this special situation?

With three children she all wanted, good jobs for both partners and a nice erotic relationship to boot?

Many of the patients I see are in such depraved relation-ships that they would be quite happy and grateful for your situation - what's going on there, between the two of you?'

Bernd: 'Yes, a lot of things have gone well for us - inclu-ding the fact that we share a good sex-life.

But since the little one was born a good three years ago, we've become more and more entangled with toxic teasings, criticism and constant arguments.

And Uta suddenly wanted to have free evenings all the time - to 'go out with the girls', allegedly, which in plain language probably meant 'with her boyfriend', as I then had to realise.

But for the sake of saving the children and our love, I could even have forgiven her, as I was still hoping for a real new beginning for us.

But Uta perceived our brilliant thousand-and-one-night encounter the other night probably more as a farewell meeting.

And now she wants us to find two smaller flats to keep the rent affordable - and that in this city, where one can hardly find any apartments!'

Still a chance for the couple?
Daniel finally offered **Uta** a therapy session for further clarification, which she accepted.

There was a creative exchange, but mainly about the formalities of the planned separation.

When in the week the children would be with whom, when the official year of separation would begin and whether one or two lawyers would be necessary?

In addition, Daniel led Uta through a *Gestalt exercise* about saying goodbye to her father when he left.

She shed a few tears during the contact with her father in this scene.

But in the end, her separation from Bernd remained.

This time was hard for **Bernd**, even when those new flats had been found rather quickly. He still hoped to win Uta back for the partnership and the family. To this end, he invited her to dinner a few times in a fancy restaurant, where they had a good time, as it seemed.

But after that, Uta distanced herself completely again. In a session with Daniel, Bernd finally realised that he had to find a new way.

Farewell letter and fire ritual
Daniel: 'Perhaps you could write Uta a farewell letter? Whatever you still want to tell her, so you can let go of this relationship in a good way. Then ignite a small fire of transformation, in the garden or by the river, and while you put this farewell letter into the fire, all the entanglements and conflicts between the two of you can dissolve in the flames at the same time.
What do you think?'

After some hesitation, **Bernd** agreed, as he felt that it was important to finally get rid of his ambivalent feelings towards Uta.

During the time of writing this farewell letter and doing the fire ritual, Bernd gradually managed to leave behind his attached feelings for Uta, as she no longer wanted a life together. Therefore he now limited his contact with her to what was necessary for raising the children together in shifts and in two apartments.

Compensatory games

Daniel had warned Bernd at this point:
'Watch out! Now that you're liberating yourself, Uta could show her ambivalent interest again!'

And indeed, a short time later, Uta did invite Bernd to a gourmet restaurant of her own accord - with an 'open end evening' - as she had never done before.

But in the meantime, also on Daniel's recommendation, Bernd had read the book *'Games People Play'* by *Eric Berne*, which made him realise that Uta and he - like many other people - were trapped in a destructive and compensatory game in which apparent closeness was rigidly combined with harsh injuries and devaluations.

'I don't have to have that anymore,' **Bernd** said to Daniel during a session. 'It hurts me because I still find her attractive - but my love for her is gone by now.
Besides, if we were to get back together as wife and husband, the year of separation would have to start all over again, because of the 'separate from table and bed rule' - and I don't want that anymore, after all that annoying back and forth!'

A cautious new beginning

This brought clarity for Bernd and his patchwork family, but it still was a difficult phase for him. During that time, he had nightmares in which his children, his parents and his ambivalent relationship with his Mom played a role.

Despite those challenges, he enjoyed the times he spent with his children and his success at work, which had now become strong anchors in Bernd's life.

At the same time, he seemed to avoid any contacts with women, who might be potential partners for him.

Daniel commented on this:

'After this difficult separation from Uta, and with that year of separation still under way, I understand very well that you are rather cautious now about a new relationship with a woman.

But how much power or influence do you still want to give to Uta in your life?

I have to ask you this, now that you've told me several times about situations in which you've more or less blocked potential contact with a young woman that was showing some interest in you.

And now again, when you were sitting in the café in the park with your friend Henry and he tried to strike up a conversation with the two nice women at the next table. Then you suddenly paid the bill and urged Henry to leave, because you allegedly had another important appointment - you're lucky, Bernd that your friend Henry doesn't tend to hold grudges!'

Bernd: 'Yes, he was a bit upset at the moment - but you know, I was just so embarrassed by the way he was contacting these women!

I just had to leave!

Besides, they weren't my type anyway.'

Daniel: 'Earlier you were talking about two nice young women. Are women in general still attractive to you? Or has the separation from Uta changed that?'

Bernd: 'Well, I'm certainly not as spontaneous as I used to be.
And will I ever be able to trust a woman again after what has happened between Uta and me?'

Homoerotic solutions
Daniel: 'Hearing you say that - what about a relationship with a man?
You had mentioned a brief homoerotic phase when you were a young man.
Could that still be relevant for you?'

Bernd: 'Well, back then it was more like trying it out with a friend, where you felt safer.
Before there was enough courage to look for girls or to arrange a date, so to speak.
But am I mainly gay because of that time?'

Daniel: 'Certainly not - there are often transition phases like that. But maybe 'bi' or bisexual, like many people?
And sometimes, a wounded relationship with a woman can be healed by a loving partnership with a man.

Of course, it doesn't have to be like that - it is only an option, and you will find the right path for yourself.

At the same time, I remember the case of a patient in this context, whom I had in therapy a few years ago.

Mind you, Bernd, this is not your story, but it is a good example, how lost or repressed personality traits can sometimes be re-integrated.

At the time, the patient was a young man in his mid-thirties who usually seemed very cautious and dejected.

Work was a secure base for him, as he had found a good position in the middle management of a financial services company.

Patient Holger

This man, whom we'll name **Holger** now, had already undergone several years of psychoanalysis plus behavioural therapy because the relationships with his women friends always broke up after a few months or years.

And that happened also, because he occasionally had very shame- and guilt-ridden affairs with rather ordinary male companions.

These previous therapies had made little difference to his 'inner turmoil'; in fact, he was now suffering from a very difficult-to-control washing compulsion, which was beginning to interfere with his otherwise problem-free working situation.'

A family's geography

Daniel: 'That's why he looked for therapy with me.

Now Holger had talked at length about his feelings of shame and guilt again, because of his homoerotic tendencies, during one session, when I suddenly had an intuition for a question.

Therefore I asked him to describe to me the layout of the rooms in his family of origin.'

Daniel: 'Maybe you could just sketch it for me, here, on this paper, who had which room and where the common rooms were.'

And **Holger** did so, after giving me quite an awake and questioning look.
This sketch then showed a flat with a kitchen-living room and a bathroom as well as three personal rooms, one each for the paternal grandmother, the mother and the father.

'And where was your room?' **I asked** him.

Holger lowered his eyes a little and said: 'Well, most of it was in the kitchen-plus-living room.
Meals, doing homework, watching TV and so on.'

'Yes, but where was your bed?
Where did you sleep?,' **I asked**.

At that moment, tears began to run down **Holger's** face as he answered:

'There was a folding bed, next to my father's bed, that's where I slept when I was seven to fifteen years old.
And he abused me as his sex partner during that time.'

With this Holger broke down completely, he cried and cried for a long time - and I gave him the roll of tissues and sat with him, touched and shocked by his story.

Tracing early trauma
When Holger had finally calmed down a little, I asked him: 'But what about your previous therapies? - You must have worked on that during your analysis, right?'

But **Holger** shook his head and said: 'No.'

'You didn't talk about these situations with your father in those therapies - how could that be?,' **Daniel** asked.

Again **Holger** shook his head and said: 'No, no.'

'Yes, but why . . .?,' **I began.**

Holger interrupted me with a wry smile: 'Nobody asked me where my room was or where my bed was during those therapies.'

After this session, Holger got better step by step.
He accepted being gay - now with inner joy and a free mind,' Daniel said to Bernd, who had listened intently to his report.
Daniel: 'When therapy had ended, Holger still kept in touch with me for a while, and during that time, he told me at some point that he had now found a boyfriend he was happy with.'

Whatever works - unconventional solutions

Quite a while later, I heard that the two of them wished for a child and therefore had teamed up with a lesbian couple they were friends with, which ultimately was successful via sperm donation.

So, that was Holger's story in a nutshell. But for you, Bernd, the question is, what options do you want to realise in your life now that you've separated from Uta - and what parts of your personality?'

'At least I had my own room,' **Bernd** said before he said goodbye to Daniel for this session.

To which **Daniel** replied:
'Yes, there you had an advantage, considering Holger.

And you understand better now, why I asked you about the layout of the rooms in your family of origin during the first few hours of therapy.'

A commentary on Holger's case
This kind of serious abuse as patient Holger had to experience it, is fortunately not so often found in therapy.

But this case is a reminder that mental and physical abuse are still taking place in way too many families, which often impedes the healthy further development of those children with a stolen childhood or youth.

Patients traumatised in this way can profit from empathic and meaningful questions in psychotherapy, so guilt and shame can transform towards healing and a new zest for life instead.

On this basis, close and long-term partnerships can often be found, where all old trauma can heal completely in the fire of love.

In therapy, it can be right to address a serious injury directly, as in Holger's case, if sharing the traumatic memories and crying over them brings relief and improvement for the patient.

In this case, the question about Holger's room and sleeping place cleared the way for his memories.

On another level of understanding, it can also be useful to ask about a sketch of *who was sitting where at the kitchen- or dining-table in the family of origin*.

This 'uncovering work' can therefore be very useful in therapy - but this approach is not equally useful for all patients. If there are signs of such resistance, the 'true and new' sentence mentioned before or one of its variants can be offered as an alternative in some cases.

Patient Bernd continued

The following sessions with **Bernd** continued to focus on his separation from Uta, on clear and friendly communication with her - and on good solutions and compromises between the two of them, for the benefit of their children.

At his working place, Bernd had now been assigned a new project as team-leader, for which he had to select the members of this team and then coach it successfully for that project.

In the therapy sessions, **Daniel** acted as a mirror and trainer for him, in order to better understand the interaction patterns and interests of his employees, as well as those of his superiors and the cooperating companies, and to be able to manage them all in a responsible and effective way.

In answer to Daniel's praise for his commitment to the company, however, **Bernd** only said: 'I'm also pleased that things are going so well with the new team and the project at work.

But I'm just missing - yes, I'm missing the right woman at my side!'

Daniel: 'It's good that you can feel that again, after this long period of letting go of Uta.

And what about your circle of friends?

Didn't you once talk about going on a bike tour, having a picnic and swimming in the lake?'

Bernd: 'Yes, I used to - but now my circle of friends and acquaintances is still evolving anew.

And I often take the children out into nature, sometimes also for a swim in one of the lakes.

Oh yes, and I've just got an invitation from the alumni group from my degree programme back then.

For a mountain hike. But with all the work to be done on this project at work, I don't know . . .'

'And that mountain tour - is it planned to happen during the week?,' **Daniel** interrupted him.

Bernd: 'No - not directly. But for a weekend plus Friday and Monday, at least, if one wants to do the whole tour.'

Daniel: 'Maybe that would be an opportunity to balance out some of your accumulated overtime?
Besides, a mountain tour with old friends is one of the best ways to renew your body and mind in nature.
Your children, your work and your own mood might benefit from it.'

A hike with friends from university days
Bernd only nodded to this, somewhat thoughtfully.
Therefore **Daniel** wondered after the end of the session whether he hadn't gone too far out on a limb with his clear 'pro mountain hike' intervention.

And he asked himself the same question again when **Bernd** greeted him only a few sessions later with the ominous words:
'You and your brilliant idea with this marvellous alumni mountain tour,' albeit with a faint smile on his face.

Nevertheless, **Daniel** was a bit worried now: 'Well then - did everyone come back safe and sound at least?'

'Yes, one could put it like that,' **Bernd** replied somewhat cryptically.

Daniel: 'That's good - but then, what was the problem? Did you have to deal with sudden shift in the weather?'

Stormy weather and its consequences
Bernd: 'Exactly, that was it!
Hurricane **Betty** swept me away!'

At **Daniel's** searching look, **Bernd** laughed:
'To be precise, her name is **Bettina** and she once studied with me at the university. At that time, we liked each other, but were both in steady relationships.
But not any more,' **Bernd** beamed at Daniel, giving him a wink of his eye.

Then, very slowly, the penny dropped in **Daniel's** blank face: 'You've found . . . ,' he began.

And **Bernd** added: 'Yes, I did!
And since then, Bettina and I are often together.
She's really good with the children - and even with Uta, amazingly enough.'
Together with Bernd, Daniel was grateful for this rather unexpected improvement.
When this situation and Bernd's mood remained stable, his therapy could be ended several sessions later.

Cynthia, a patient at risk
Now we'll continue with patient **Cynthia**, this young woman with *Anorexia* and suicidal thoughts that **Daniel** had mentioned above already.

Cynthia had insisted on 'no medications' in the first trial sessions with Daniel, which wasn't easy for him.

Contracts at the beginning of therapy
Nevertheless, he finally accepted patient **Cynthia** for a short-term therapy of twelve sessions.
Before that, however, he'd made an agreement on two conditions for therapy with this patient.
One was that Cynthia would call him or the MVZ *before* she planned or carried out any self-harming measures.
For this, she was given an emergency number with permanent on-call service.

The second condition **Daniel** agreed upon with Cynthia before therapy was the commitment that she would only quit her present workplace, when she at least had signed a preliminary contract for a new position.
And that before filing her notice for the present job.

This second condition was important to Daniel, because he saw that her work was providing a secure basis for Cynthia's life, even though she often complained about the heavy workload and her unfriendly colleagues at the company.

As **Cynthia** understood those conditions and agreed to both of them, therapy could begin.
The first few sessions went well, with Cynthia practising appreciative perception and communication skills, while she was gradually gaining confidence in this work.

Problems at work

But then a conflict arose at the company.

A superior, with whom Cynthia had problems already, made an inappropriate comment about Cynthia's 'lithe and lissom appearance', which initially had triggered a *bulimic vomiting* bout in the patient.

In a fit of anger over this incident, **Cynthia** eventually quit her job in the heat of her emotions - without thinking about her contracts in therapy.

Daniel said to her: 'This was agreed otherwise between us, but I do understand that you didn't want to work for this boss any longer.

Besides, you've been planning to find a more suitable job for quite some time. And now you also have a good reason that motivates you to do so!'

Cynthia agreed to this and therefore let **Daniel** help her with appropriate exercises and role plays in writing her applications and to prepare for future job interviews.

And her chances of finding a suitable job on the market were good, especially as she had received a fine reference from her last employer, based on her performance at the company.

Withdrawal tendencies

But then **Cynthia** suddenly began to develop strong guilt feelings about her sudden quitting of her job at the company - intense guilt pangs that were hard to understand for all others.

She withdrew more and more into her room in the living community - sometimes even into her children's room in the house of her parents.

Daniel was alarmed at this development, therefore he said to her:

'Cynthia, this conflict and emotional distance between your parents that you've mentioned - this very tense situation is not doing you any good.

Your parents need to resolve these problems by and for themselves.

Perhaps in a couple's therapy programme?'

Cynthia: 'My Mom and I have already tried steps in that direction many times - but my Dad doesn't believe in therapy!'

Daniel: 'If that's the case, it's all the more true that this area of conflict between your parents is a stressful one for you.

Find your own purpose in life - and above all, find the right job, because that will boost your self-confidence and help you to financially stand on your own two feet again!'

Cynthia felt the same way, which is why she wanted to actively tackle her job search now. Then, however, she cancelled the next session with Daniel due to a cold.

At the following appointment with Daniel, Cynthia now appeared even thinner and paler than he already knew her, with pronounced dark circles under her eyes.

Inner turmoil

Daniel asked: 'Are you all right?

You look a bit under the weather, as it seems?'

Cynthia answered: 'I'm so sorry - I've just done it again,' then she burst into tears.

After a while, she told Daniel that she had gone back to her room in the living community after a weekend with her parents. There, nothing seemed to make sense to her anymore, so she ended up taking 'lots of pills'.

As with her previous attempt, back then, at her parents' house, she was found in time, this time by her flatmates, who took her to the clinic.

Daniel: 'But why didn't you call me?'

Cynthia: 'I simply forgot!'

At the same time, Cynthia asked Daniel to continue therapy sessions with her, as the first part of short-term therapy was nearing its end now.

Daniel said: 'First of all, thank you for your trust in our work - and that you want to continue it.

And maybe that will be possible still.

But at the moment, and despite all my empathy for your difficult situation, I must also face the fact that by now you've broken both of the contracts that we had made before we started therapy, which has resulted in very serious consequences.

What serves the patient?

Considering all this, I can no longer justify therapy as the only approach, especially as we now have discussed the options of several medications a number of times, which you have always refused so far.

But as long as you haven't at least tried an anti-depressive, mood stabilising treatment with *a nasal spray containing Ketamine®* or with therapeutically supervised *Ketamine® infusions*, it is simply too dangerous to go on just with psychotherapy alone.'

Cynthia was not so happy about Daniel's decision, but she understood his arguments.
And a few weeks later, she contacted him again.

Motivated by the strong pressure of suffering in her life, Cynthia had finally found the courage to follow Daniel's advice.

Initially, she was prescribed a *Ketamine® nasal spray*, which already improved her mood enough so she could start looking for job offers again.

Depression treatment with Ketamine®
Due to the good results with the nasal spray, Cynthia then decided to undergo *Ketamine® infusion therapy* as an outpatient in a psychiatric practice, consisting of 3-6 45-minute infusion sessions, accompanied by therapy.

At the next meeting with **Daniel**, he was soon feeling the change in her stance and aura.

Cynthia: 'It was a bit as if the light switch in my brain had finally been switched on again!

Especially during the infusions - but it still has a positive effect on my mood and my outlook on life.'

In the course of these experiences, Cynthia realised very directly, to which extent her anorexia, her bulimic attacks and her current refusal to work and to live were interwoven and entangled with the frozen conflict between her parents.

Possible couples therapy
She therefore had decided from the bottom of her heart that she wanted to shape and enjoy her life in an independent and self-directed way from now on.
Even though she still wished her parents healing and all the best.

In addition, **Daniel** had given her the telephone number of an experienced senior couples' therapist.

'He's quite down to earth and might perhaps be able to reach your father, even if he sometimes seems a bit strange or cranky,' he had said.
During the time of another twelve sessions in the second part of short-term therapy, Cynthia was able to gradually distance herself from her self-harming behaviour.

Her bulimic vomiting attacks reduced step by step, while her interest in the good things in life was beginning to increase again.

Cynthia: 'I can hardly believe it myself - but I've found something like an appetite for life again, yes actually, an appetite for life,' she explained to Daniel in one of the last sessions. It was the meeting, in which she had previously described to him, how well her new company and her job there were just 'made for her'.

Daniel was grateful for Cynthia's progress. In addition, he gave her some book references for further personal development. See *Bibliography*.

So much - or so little - about the three patients Daniel had mentioned to his partner and colleague Cordula a while ago.

True and new Reloaded

And so back to Cordula and her strange sentence, which, in a modified form, also happened to be a useful turning point for Daniel's patient **Cynthia**.

During the second part of therapy, **Daniel** had offered her the following exercise: 'Imagine that you hear yourself saying as if from far away:

'Dearest Mom, I know it's not new,
but to you I'll stay forever true!'
And:
'Dearest Dad, I know it's not new,
but to you I'll stay forever true!'

A while after she had worked with those sentences in therapy, **Cynthia** started contacting and meeting people from her circle of friends again.

'True and new' in supervision part II

But how did **Cordula** continue with this 'true and new' sentence just mentioned, especially during the next meeting with **'Dr Jones'**, as she inwardly called her supervisor?
Right at the beginning of this supervision session, he immediately asked her a question:
'Have you applied this sentence from our last conference to others than your patient Ernst?'

Unexpected effects
And **Cordula** replied in the negative.
Then **'Dr Jones'** said:
'But I did - ashes on my head!
Then the patient threw a violent anger tantrum, which nearly demolished my practice.'
Cordula: 'Oh dear - yes, that is possible.
Anyhow, did you happen to have a *bioenergetics stool* or something like that on hand?
In such a case, hitting the stool with a suitable bat can express and transform the aggression, when the patient is encouraged appropriately. -
But who was your patient so angry at to begin with?'

Martin, a patient with obsessive-compulsive disorder
'Dr Jones': 'Especially his mother. This patient, I'll call him **Martin** here, is otherwise an over-correct and very disciplined man, who is suffering from several disturbing washing, cleaning and controlling compulsions.

These compulsions, as well as communication problems in his family and at work, had brought him into therapy. To summarise the situation briefly, Martin hails from a family that lost the father in an accident many years ago. The patient therefore grew up with his mother, his aunt and his paternal grandmother, together with his sister, who is two years younger than him and had been conceived shortly before their father's death.

Unfortunately, his mother and aunt in particular used Martin from an early age as sort of a lightning rod for their difficult experiences with men, against which he, as the little boy in this female-dominated family, could hardly defend himself. Only sometimes his little sister and his grandmother helped him a bit.

Challenges in the family of origin
We had worked on this traumatic situation a number of times, also with the help of his dreams. But Martin is a special kind of a patient - how can I put this? -
He is practically 'on last name basis' with himself, in his constant endeavours to do everything right and to control all he is doing and his environment.
But so far, he hardly had any contact with his feelings, which he has learnt to repress even as a child.
And I thought that this paradoxical sentence of yours might be useful in his situation - and then this ordeal!
Rarely have I seen someone so angry - and no, I didn't have a *bioenergetics stool;* but it's probably a good idea for such cases.

In the end, I offered him a big cushion to hit - and old phone books to tear up. This allowed him to destroy the damaging aspects of his mother in his imagination.
That felt right for Martin, but he also was exhausted, had sore muscles in his shoulders and was sad.'

Emotional work
Cordula: 'But that's a good result for your patient, all in all considered.'

'Dr Jones': 'Do you think so?
He was rather confused when he left.
And I myself certainly had some doubts, whether the exercise with this sentence really was such a good thing for him.
Violent cathartic processes or emotional outbursts of this strength are normally rather rare in my mostly analytical work - so it was simply a bit unusual for me.'

Cordula: 'But isn't that exactly what therapy is about, a lot of the time, enabling people to regain access to their feelings, which often were repressed very early in their childhood?'

'Dr Jones': 'But maybe not at the expense of the practice furniture, if possible?!'

Cordula: 'I'm really sorry that you had to face such an emotional charge in your patient, when you tried that 'true and new' sentence for the first time.

But why don't you wait and see how things will go for Martin? Because by now you've freed him of his emotional shackles, while you were there for him in the hour of his anger and his grief.

Perhaps this will help him in finding the other emotional pole in himself as well, the ability to share close and tender moments.'

New and true: When, how and for whom?

Cordula then reported on her experiences with the 'true and new' sentences in her work with her patient Ernst: 'If one explains this sentence first, by telling the patient that it primarily serves to appreciate and integrate the inner child's early loyalty to suffering parents, then most patients will accept this work.

And any kind of irony is completely out of place in this sensitive context!

Therefore we should only use this sentence, if we can say it to the patient in a friendly and empathic way.'

'Dr Jones': 'I'm sure you're right, that's the only way to guide it towards a constructive and healing process.

But how do you proceed with the severely traumatised patients, like Martin for example - or with people who refuse to say the sentence in the *Empty Chair setting?*'

Cordula: 'Yes, these are exactly the questions I have been dealing with since this 'true and new' sentence has emerged. Another question that needs to be considered in each case is the following:

'When in the course of therapy does it make sense to use this tool?'

To this, **'Dr Jones'** nodded with the faintest smile and **Cordula** continued: 'We can still discuss these questions, because caution and the precise selection of patients and timing are necessary with this partly paradoxical instrument in order to ensure a safe framework for all of our patients.

Indications
But tell me, have you tried this sentence for yourself already?'

In response, **'Dr Jones'** blinked several times while his eyes made rapid movements to the top left and right. Then he replied: 'You more or less know that already, because you yourself have told me that verse in our last session.'

Cordula: 'Yes, I remember. You briefly went into a mild therapeutic trance state, during which you have perhaps experimented with this sentence for yourself internally, with your own parents?'

'Dr Jones': 'That's exactly how it was. And it amazed me how directly that simple verse connected me to some decisive memories from my early years, some of which I had worked on in my teaching analysis.
Hence my optimism last time, when you first told me about this 'true and new' sentence.
But then, I wasn't sitting on such an explosive emotional charge as Martin, for example.'

Cordula: 'Yes, it's good that you have done so much work on yourself already, so it's safer to use such a deliberately paradoxical tool. And there are some situations in which this 'true and new' sentence towards the parents can also be contraindicated.'

Contraindications
'Dr Jones' looked at her with a questioning eye.

Cordula: 'Yes, my partner and colleague Daniel and I clarified that in our discussions on this subject.
For example, *if a parent has taken their own life or has died early on in an accident or through serious illness, this sentence should not be used.*

Possible variants of the sentence
And with severely traumatised, often very emotionally congested patients like your Martin or some borderline patients, there are ways of softening the sentence, so that violent anger outbursts like your patient's can be avoided in most cases.

For example, you can explain to a patient that she sees both herself and the parent to whom she says the 'new and true' sentence in her imagination as if 'from far away' while she is saying the sentence.

If this is still too difficult, the patient can imagine a pane of frosted glass that is placed in between to create a safe distance.

And it is possible to abandon this whole *Gestalt setting* with the *Empty Chair* plus - usually - a mother or father.
This is done by asking the patient:
'How do you feel, when you hear yourself saying the following sentence, as if you heard it from far away?'
The sentence is then offered to the patient.
But even with this simplified form we should better be prepared for any possible reaction.

Effects in silence
Which brings us to your question from before, about the patients who only want to say this sentence to one of their parents or not at all.
This must always be accepted, otherwise the therapeutic process will finish in a cul-de-sac or dead end road that is caused by a superfluous power struggle.
But the sentence can be explained in a way that ensures that this conflict doesn't arise in the first place.'

'Dr Jones': 'That sounds quite interesting - but how is it supposed to work in therapeutic practice?'

Cordula: 'Above all, by offering the option of only saying the sentence inwardly and silently or of just hearing it, and that right at the beginning of this work.
So if I had a patient to whom I had explained that this strange paradoxical sentence serves to appreciate and better integrate their own childlike loyalty to problem-entangled parents, then I would guide this patient may-be like this:

'If you want, you can say this 'true and new' sentence directly and out loud to your mother or father now, with me as a witness, which helps most patients.

But sometimes the effects might even be better if this magic sentence is only said internally and in silence.
Or if the sentence is just heard, as if you were saying it yourself, but from far, far away.

This could be the offer to avoid conflicts with the direct use of this sentence in the *Empty Chair setting.*'

'Dr Jones': 'Chapeau! Hats off!
An elegant win-win solution for the patient - and you as the therapist can remain centered now, no matter which option the patient decides for.

Yes, these additions to and changes of the sentence itself, as well as in the general setting that you've just mentioned adapt this tool more precisely to the needs of the individual patient. That encourages me to carefully keep using this sentence with some of my patients.'

Easy does it
Cordula: 'Yes, carefulness is very important here.
Because this paradoxical 'new and true' sentence can sometimes be like a *'passe-partout'*, a kind of universal key that enables suffering people to make very direct contact, consciously or unconsciently, with the decisive scenes of their childhood and adolescence.

And even if these variations of the sentence and of its setting make the application safer, the contraindications remain, which are repeated here once again:

If, for example, a parent has taken their own life or died early in an accident or through serious illness, it is better not to use this sentence.

And despite all caution in its use, we must always face the fact that such a paradoxical and directly regression-promoting sentence as this 'true and new' sentence can also trigger outbursts of anger and tears in some people, as you have experienced it with your patient.'

'Dr Jones': 'The Bioenergetics stool plus fitting bat is on my to-do list already.

And maybe we also have to reckon with the fact that the application of this sentence occasionally could shorten the necessary duration of therapy.

But does that make any sense?'

Cordula: 'A short poem appears in my mind as we are talking about this question.'

Why?

*That is the deepest meaning far and wide
in this amazing roller-coaster ride:*

*It is the way it is - that is in-herent
Unless perhaps - it is diff-erent.*

The round table

Participants in a theology or psychology seminar are told by their teachers that on this day there will be practical self-experience through personal observation of special field studies.

Then they hear the announcement:

'The first thing you see here is hell.'

Through a one-way mirror, as is sometimes also used in family therapy, the seminar participants look at a group of people sitting around a table. In the centre of the table is a large pot of delicious food.

And the people sitting around the table all have rather long spoons with which they are trying to get the good food out of the pot in the centre of the table - and into their mouths.

But because everyone is doing this individually and all at the same time, the long spoons get tangled up, the food falls down and loud arguments arise.

Then the participants are led further to another one-way mirror.

At first glance, the room behind it looks almost exactly the same as the room just before. Only that it's quieter here. Then they hear the message:

'Look. This is a glance at heaven.'

And now they see it:

Those long spoons are here too, but this time people are using them to feed each other.

New. An Epilogue

Couples
Would you mind being kind?

So what is the result now of this small collection of case studies?
You have learnt about some methods and therapeutic approaches that can be useful for the improvement and healing of psychological disorders.
In real practice, the spectrum of all people undergoing therapy is of course much wider than in the cases we've reported on in this text.

Patients of all ages and from all walks of life
If we assume that growing babies, who are living in their mother's womb, are particularly open and receptive to all impressions from outside, then they are among the youngest patients in therapy.
Babies, children and adolescents
Then there are the children and adolescents who are 'taking care of their parents' for very good reasons, by becoming mentally or physically ill, by their school or educational performance collapsing, or by simply 'not managing' to move out of their parents' home on a permanent basis.

As a therapist, it is understandable to try to encourage the young 'nest-sitter' to progressively cope with life by moving out soon and completing her education.

And yet in the middle of a therapeutic 'cul-de-sac' or dead end road.

Even though the therapist had motivated the patient correctly, as one might think.

Validating the child's efforts to stabilise the family

Yes, the patient certainly needs motivation to be more independent, but above all else, she needs to be recognised and appreciated for her contribution to the family.

For some children and adolescents, it can be very difficult to detach themselves from home and then start their own lives, in the face of their quarrelling or distant parents, often because of an 'extinguished fireplace' in their life.

In addition to understanding and empathy - as well as asking questions and listening thoroughly - the 'new and true' sentence can be of therapeutic value here as well.

Courtship - The phase of choosing a partner for life

Then the many young people before or at the beginning of a partnership, who - also because of the challenging families of origin they have experienced themselves - are struggling with *strong ambivalences* regarding a stable relationship, flowing intimacy and a possible future role as a parent.

House cleaning in therapy

Sometimes this is the case, because certain events, such as the separation of the parents or the early death of a sibling, need to be dealt with and integrated in therapy before the commitment upon a long-term partnership or marriage can be dared.

Suffering couples and families

And then there is the 'multifaceted theme with so many variations', regarding patients in difficult, unhappy or crisis-ridden relationships, in many cases after a child or two, with a flat or house mortgage, and mostly with a lot of stress at work.

Therapy can be helpful in these situations as well - if it is not 'too late' already for a particular couple, because their separating centrifugal forces, often fuelled by retrograde loyalties to the parents, have grown too strong for too long already.

Forms of couples therapy

Also in cases, where there has been an external relationship by one of the partners, this can be a great challenge for the couple in finding their way back to stable trust and loving intimacy again.

If couples in such a crisis or in pre-separation situations are still willing to give their partnership a new chance, individual and couples therapy can be useful to work through and let go of old baggage, as seen in the case histories, but also to support the couple in rediscovering mutual appreciation, recognition and tenderness.

Long live the present!

All of the wisdom and love traditions of humanity tell us that gratitude and happiness can only be found in the present moment.

Mindfulness exercises and times of shared meditation create new meeting spaces for those couples who want to explore them.

Loving intimacy

Dear reader,

If you happen to belong to one of the fortunate couples who are completely satisfied with their love life, you can skim over the next few lines.

However, depending on the statistics, only 16 to 60% of all couples are really satisfied with their sexuality.

In other words: 40 - 84% of all couples are suffering from *anhedonia*, denoting a pathological lack of pleasure in their intimacy, as seen in the case studies already.

Therefore the question arises, how couples, who are still motivated to do so, can escape this insidious anhedonia, which often is only noticed late by the couple, and how they can instead find their way back to a flowing and loving intimacy in their relationship.

Talking about personal needs and desires

As trivial as this may sound, but you might have to face the fact that your partner doesn't master all possible telepathic abilities quite yet.

That's why it helps a lot, if you simply are talking with each other, on the way back to closeness and shared joy: 'This feels good to me - and that doesn't.'

As simple as this may seem, as we have seen, it is rather difficult for many couples, considering that sexuality is still a taboo subject for many and that there often are ingrained patterns of distance and arguments, which have replaced loving closeness.

Letting go of inner walls and arguments
Then it is a real challenge to give up any of the apparent power-position that lasting icy silence or hotly escalating conflicts would have enabled otherwise.
Couples, however, who succeed in ending this old bad game of mutual devaluation and hurt also stand to gain a great value.
Because the energy that was previously channelled into arguments and contempt can now be utilized in other areas by the partners.

Inviting loving closeness and orgiastic gardens
Even if it is hard to believe in today's internet age with erotic formats everywhere from magazine newsstands to Tinder® to You-Tube®:
Far too many people don't even have sex with themselves. This way, regular practise gets lost, which often makes couples' love-life more difficult and frequently leads to avoidance of intimacy.

Yet, for example, if a woman has learnt how to reach a climax for herself, then she is able to take her happiness into her own hands as well, when she is in loving union with her partner.
This requires a man as her partner, however, who has learnt to put his orgasm reflex on hold, at least for a while.
Male orgasm and its timing
For some men, this control over their orgasm reflex is an innate ability - chapeau! Hats off!

The vast majority of masculinity, however, are not so fortunate and therefore have to make do by training 'practising procedures'.
Here are just some of the main options.

1) *'Play it again, Sam.' 'We'll try it again.'* In other words: The man has already had a climax - the night before or a few hours ago.

Then, when the couple comes together again, the man usually has a longer stamina, which means he can accompany and support his partner much better on her way into her orgiastic or poly-orgiastic gardens.

2) *'The man learns to surf with high energy'*
This means that men also practise during masturbation to let their arousal build up until shortly before orgasm - and then to allow the erection subside again.

To practise this kind of 'containment', which really is an exercise of collection, more regularly and repeatedly, will significantly improve reflex control over time.
Just a matter of motivation, man!

3) *'Calming herbs or medications'*
These include valerian and creams containing Lidocaine® - sparingly! - for the penis.

4) *'How about music in your bedroom?'*
A stereo set, a candle and an inspiring scent . . .

Finding the source together
5) *'The basic tantric position'*
Well-known, rarely used. The woman lies on her back, the man usually on his left side.
Advantage: both are relaxed and have free hands.
6) *'A creative pause'*
This exercise, which is quite simple in itself, requires the man to train his mindfulness at the same time.
This enables him to notice in good time when his orgasm reflex is beginning to build up. That gives him the chance to offer his partner a pause in their embrace until the excitement has calmed down again.
Through such precisely sensed pauses in their loving embrace, the couple gains the important freedom of a longer and peaceful union.
7) *'In the face of the Great You'*
This is a fundamental element that can help a couple to meet and melt in a new way.
This refers to a very meditative attitude in intimacy, through which the couple finds the original source of love during their union.

If these experiences are dared again, or explored for the first time, this will help to revitalise estranged relation-ships, avoid unnecessary separations and enable lasting and loving stability for all the families involved.
Perhaps that would be worth the effort. And we can remember that we have already learnt how to ride a bike, which is also about constant control to keep the right balance. This skill can be built upon.

Often, however, a couple's willingness or ability to be close and intimate is so damaged and blocked that some further interventions are necessary to support improvement or even healing in those cases.

This indicates the controlled, medically supervised use of Psycho-Active Substances, or **PAS** for short.

The fact that some of these PAS could also be used as aphrodisiacs to make effective help available to suffering couples has *so far* hardly been recognised in therapy and medicine.

Psycho-Active Substances = PAS in couples therapy

For instance the **Cannabis** plant, which unfortunately is often 'decried' unscientifically by the medical profession even today, is now proving to be a genuine remedy in many areas of medicine - and for emotionally estranged couples as well.

The mild PAS **Ibogaine** is a natural anti-depressant that can also be of help here in micro doses in the evening. *Ibogaine* is freely available in some countries.

The substance **MDMA**, which was used in therapy in the 1970-80s already, then named **Empathy** or compassion, for group and individual sessions as well as for couples, is even more beneficial in 'healing estranged relations'.

Now MDMA was approved for controlled medical use in Australia in 2023, the first country in the world to dare this important step.

Then approval by the FDA in the USA was expected on August 11, 2024, thanks above all to the tireless efforts of *Rick Doblin, Ph.D.* and the non-profit organisation *MAPS*, which he had founded in 1986.

In the end, however, and despite *two Phase III studies* on successful PTSD treatment with MDMA conducted by MAPS - a panel of alleged 'experts' at the FDA in the US decided otherwise.

Right in the face of tons of scientific evidence!

So much fear of real healing and love. Therefore:

Book *'Alice'* on Psycho-Active Substances in individual, couples and group therapy

You can find more information on the application of *PAS in psychotherapy* in our book: *'Alice - through fire and water'* and in the articles: *'Peace can be learned!'* and *'Quo vadis, humanitas?'*, see *Bibliography*.

One more PS in this context:

In the hour lies the power
Almost all tasks
that can be completed in a short time,
can also be fulfilled
in a much longer time.

Is the healing potential of PAS wanted by politics?
This path of controlled medical application of suitable PAS in therapy could fundamentally help many patients, couples and families - as soon as the political will is there to let this happen.

Is the peace potential of PAS wanted by politics?
And if applied worldwide, these PAS would help to make it much more difficult for those severely traumatised, pathologically egomaniac autocrats to come to power in the future.

Because voters, who have gained insight by their own experience, would hardly vote people into leadership positions any longer, who haven't yet experienced PAS for themselves.

This may sound idealistic or utopian.

Nevertheless, the following holds true:

People, who have had such heart- and soul-opening experiences in an appropriate setting, are usually no longer starting any fires.

Instead, they help to extinguish them.

Senior patients

Yes, and then there are the aged, older and senior patients, who sometimes apply for psychotherapy also.

Patient **Rita**, for example, in her early sixties, from a wealthy family, married and mother of four grown-up children, who is asking for an appointment with doctor and psychotherapist **Cordula** due to several depressive symptoms and anxiety attacks.

But Cordula can hardly find any real problems or areas of conflict in **Rita's** life, while she is writing up her case history.

On the contrary, the dynamic and much younger-looking patient tells Cordula about various exclusive hobbies that she and her husband now have more time for after his retirement as a senior manager in the industrial area.

For example, horse-riding, flying motorised hang-gliders or jet-skiing in the ocean.

She does complain, however, about relatively frequent conflicts with her husband, when they are discussing the development and education of their children.

A happy older couple

When Cordula asks her whether she also shares good times with her husband - apart from these hobbies - for example in their love-life, Rita replies that she and her husband can live this area in a good and fulfilling way.

And **Cordula** congratulates her on this.

But then the patient recounted *a dream from one of the last nights* in which her two daughters had fallen ill, which really worried her in her dream.

Directing a dream in the waking state

Under Cordula's guidance, Rita looked at possible problem- and solution-variants of her dream, learning like this how she can direct all the developments in her own dreams while being awake.

Due to the patient's repeated complaints about these unnerving arguments with her husband, the therapist finally asked her, whether a session with her husband might be useful in this context?

A session with the patient's partner

As **Rita** agreed to this, an appointment was also made with **Hubert**, her husband.

In that session, **Cordula** asked him to help her find possible ways to improve and heal his wife's depressive mood and her anxiety attacks.

Hubert, himself in his mid-sixties and looking a bit sad, was more than willing to do so.

But when Cordula complimented him about the fulfilling intimacy with his wife, he only raised his shoulders and shook his head.

Cordula: 'Why is that now? Your wife told me that you share a beautiful and successful intimacy?

Maybe you can explain that to me?'

A good love-life?

Hubert: 'Yes, it was okay, kind of, in our younger years, somehow.

And it certainly was enough for all of our children . . .'

Cordula: 'But?'

Hubert: 'Well, you know, it always was a difficult thing - because Rita never was able to reach a climax for herself.'

My mother once told me

When **Cordula** asked **Rita** about this situation in their next session, she explained: 'My mother told me in my youth that an orgasm wasn't such an important thing for women.

By which she probably meant that men are dominating everything already - why should we women throw that at them, too?'

Cordula was shocked by this reduced love energy over such a long time. Therefore she tried to encourage Rita and Hubert in a couple's session to dare a fresh start in their relationship. The result remained open.

Love needs courage
Why exactly this case report right now, towards the end of this text? This is done hoping that you, dear reader, don't have to discover at some point:
'Oh - there is something wonderful that we could have shared - if we only had allowed ourselves to do it!'

But way too often, we prefer to stick to **Karl Valentin** and his timeless motto, here first given in strongly Bavarian German, then translated into English:

'Meng hätt ma scho wolln -
Aba dürfn hamma uns ned traut!'

Approximate translation:
'Liking we might have wanted -
But letting us we didn't dare!'
But as original and precise as this well-known quote by *Karl Valentin* is outlining the frequent complexes in the area of closeness and intimacy, we could ask ourselves an additional question still:
'Do we want to keep our lives that way?'
Appreciating loving intimacy
The above case report should also inspire us to finally end all devaluation of loving partnerships with a flowing and orgiastic intimacy for both.
A devaluation that sometimes is passed on by parents to their children even today, who then are suffering from this blocked love energy in similar ways as their parents did before.

Healing Thou, healing you
Because only by learning or relearning the loving 'you-I'
and 'I-you' between woman and woman, woman and
man and man and man - as well as, in an appropriate
form, between parents and children - can the crises and
wars between couples, families and nations be solved on
a permanent basis.

Old age
And some older and very old patients are occasionally
also interested in doing psychotherapy.
Amongst other reasons, this is, because in this period,
from around the 60's to the 80's to the 108's, in this
advanced phase of life 'the blows are striking closer', as
the saying goes.

To begin with, the more or less abrupt end of a long
professional career with all the corresponding results -
'Papa ante Portas'*, for example.
*A German film-comedy on 'Papa's Retirement' directed by
Victor von Bülow, also known as the unforgettable *'Loriot'*.

But then also physical, age-related limitations and
illnesses - and finally the ever-closer 'leave-takings' of
relatives and friends, or of well-known, familiar figures
from public life, such as the arts, politics and sport.

Patients with a recently deceased partner
A patient, who is in his 60s or 70s and who has lost his
beloved wife a while ago, is asking **Daniel** for therapy.

This patient, who is called **Paul** here, continues to work as an electrician in the industry, which gives him a stable living situation.

But the fight against his wife's aggressive cancer, with the many stressful side effects of her medication, plus the pain caused by the disease itself, had left a heavy mark on the previously cheerful and optimistic father of three grown-up children.

During therapy, the **patient** said to Daniel: 'I am grateful for our children. And in the phase when my wife **Helga** was getting worse and worse, they really helped me. They are lovely children.

But they all have a lot to do at work and some of them have several small children of their own, so there's not much time left, not least because our families are living quite far apart at the moment.

And my depressive mental carousels, with this chaos in the house, are of course not so appealing to my children either.'

With these words, the shadows of sadness, resignation and despair deepened again on **Paul's** face.

Only when **Daniel** happened upon the idea of asking him for a picture of his late wife, that a brief though timid smile appeared in the patient's eyes.

On the screen of the smartphone, Daniel saw a powerful smiling and attractive woman in her prime.
Therefore he once again gave his condolences to **Paul**.

Daniel: 'Now I've got a better understanding for your situation. This was a profound and lasting love between you and your wife Helga.
So it hurts all the more to let go.'
Now **Paul** began to open up to the dialogue with Daniel and told him the story of Helga and Paul and their family, while he was laughing and crying.

After a while, **Daniel** even was able to interest the self-declared non-reader Paul in a book: ***'Trusting life anew'***, by **Elisabeth Kübler-Ross** and **David Kessler**.
See *Bibliography*.

A farewell letter with fire ritual at the riverside
Later, he also wrote a farewell letter to his deceased wife, which then was burnt - and thus 'delivered' - in a fire next to the river.

Very slowly, the paralysing grief began to recede from **Paul's** mind and feelings.
And as spring arrived, he gradually reconnected with his circle of friends, at bowling, in the church community and in a dance café that he knew from earlier days.
Therapy could be ended, when the patient was making plans for a longer summer vacation, together with some friends in a travel group.

Herbert, a patient with psychiatric diagnosis
Another senior patient that Daniel had worked with was
Herbert, in his late seventies, who had lost his wife in an
accident many years ago.
He had been a successful graduate engineer in industrial
mechanical engineering, but had been forced to give up
that profession in his early sixties, because he had
developed increasing mental problems with delusional
ideas, which ultimately were diagnosed as *schizophrenia*
and treated with *anti-psychotic medication.*

The patient was living in an assisted living community,
where he usually coped well with low-dose medication
to prevent relapses.

As he had recently become more depressed, however,
and was disturbing his flatmates with 'strange ideas', an
appointment was made for therapy.

But when Daniel was reading the patient's age on the
referral form, plus his diagnosis: *'Schizophrenic residual',*
which means 'remaining schizophrenic state', he initially
wasn't so sure, whether any therapeutic work would still
make sense in this case.

When he then first met the patient in person, he was
surprised to find an older gentleman with snow-white
hair all right, but who otherwise kept himself in a very
upright manner and made contact easily, which was not
a matter of course, considering his diagnosis.

Only when Daniel asked him about his problems and what he hoped to achieve in therapy, the situation was getting clearer. **Herbert**, the patient, now began to fantasise and confabulate 'the blue out of the sky'.

Fantastic tales
'Yes, yes, Doctor, it's no longer safe in our living community - there's a really dangerous burner in the basement of our house - and that's exactly why I called the fire brigade.

And the flooding of Ulrike's flat on the third floor didn't help either, but they didn't let me call the police, our friends and helpers.
Except - except when they are watching you!
Yes, some obscure people from the FBI, BBC and CIA are on my heels . . .'

At this point, **Daniel** interrupted his wild story with the following comment:
'Good thing you were paying attention, regarding the fire and the flooding!,' which earned him half a smile, together with a surprisingly direct look from the patient.

Who is pursuing the patient
'And as far as those control freaks from CIA and the like go - a colleague of mine had a patient with quite similar stalking problems a while ago.
This patient now was sure of being followed by several people whenever he left his apartment.

But that made his life very difficult, because he always had to take precautions to shake off his pursuers.'
Here Daniel made a pause, while his patient **Herbert** nodded in agreement.

Now **Daniel** continued:
'Then this patient, who felt stalked all the time, went to a therapist because of his increasingly difficult life situation. This colleague first listened to his story at length and in peace.

How to outwit persistent stalkers
But then, together with the patient, he began to develop particularly suitable strategies to mislead any potential pursuers and controllers in order to shake them off effectively.
And in the beginning, the patient participated in an engaged way - no therapist or doctor had ever helped him like this before - but as the plans for when and where he should change bikes, underground trains, buses and other means of transport as quickly as possible, were getting ever more complex and time-consuming, his strong 'enthusiasm to avoid stalkers' was gradually waning.

The therapist behind the curtain
But it was only when the patient found the therapist next to the window and behind the curtain at the beginning of the next session that a turning point in their therapeutic work was getting closer.

Therapist: 'Today I saw it for myself - that guy over there was on your heels.
And now he's waiting there at the corner of the street.'

But by the time the **patient** had walked to the window, nobody could be seen at that street corner.

'Those stalkers are very clever guys,' the **colleague** had commented on this.
As a result, it became ever less important to this patient whether someone was following or stalking him.
Instead, his work in therapy now turned to other topics.

Herbert had listened with interest to this case report by Daniel. Now he was more receptive to Daniel's questions about his living situation, his hobbies and the circle of friends in his life.
During that short term therapy, Herbert borrowed two books on the subject of family therapy from the library in the waiting room of the MVZ or medical care center.
One was *'Zweierlei Glück'* or: *'Two kinds of happiness'* by *Gunthard Weber*, which describes **Bert Hellinger's** work with **Family Constellations.**

And the other: **'Circular Questioning'** by *Christel Rech-Simon* and *Fritz Simon*, on the subject of family therapy as well.
Reading these books eventually enabled him to clarify and resolve some 'unfinished business' from the history of his life in his therapy.

Sense in nonsense

It is one thing in particular, however, that should be remembered from this case report on **Herbert** and his *'schizophrenic residual'*:

Which is that it is sometimes - not always! - possible to establish a functional working relationship in therapy even with delusional patients.

If the therapist is prepared to at least partially address the presented, seemingly completely nonsensical and delusional ideas - 'It's good that you paid attention when the fire and the flood happened!' - Because this first of all interrupts the hallucinated flight of ideas, which allows for personal contact and then for an exchange about the real issues to be worked on. Because:

tool
The words of the Fool
on the Hill, dreaming there still
are often a helpful tool
as children's speak will -
these words are fast swept away
yet to truth they might point you the way.

Prevention: Fast food, tobacco, alcohol and company

Another issue that some patients have to deal with when they reach older age, are the long-term effects of an unbalanced diet, with too much meat, fat, sugar and fast food, as well as alcohol, tobacco, TV and internet consumption.

Unfortunately, the *metabolic syndrome* in old age with obesity, diabetes, hypertension and elevated blood lipids is often difficult to treat, because vital organs such as the liver and kidneys, then lungs, heart and vascular system plus brain are too damaged already.

A timely focus
Therefore it is all the more important to start active prevention with patients of a younger age already.

This way, an impulse can be created in those younger people - be it in a therapy or in a conversation among friends - which ultimately may lead to stepwise reducing or ending an abusive consumption.

And this in turn lays the foundation for a healthier, fitter and mentally more present life, including senior age.

Trainings for life
Therefore, we should, for example, approach the young smoker and inform her about nicotine patches, about non-smoking *DIGAS*, denoting *digital health applications* and about non-smoking self-help and support groups.

Drinking and good health?
The same goes for helping a younger man who wants to control his excessive drinking behaviour, as there are useful medications, DIGAS and self-help groups for this situation as well.

Besides, strategies are needed for utilizing the energy and time that is set free when smoking and drinking are reduced or eliminated.

For example, all forms of sport, creative work or outings into nature.

Addiction understood as compensatory behaviour

It is good to remember in this context, that practically all addictions, compulsions or clinging tendencies can be seen as *compensatory behaviours*, intended to replace and thus to compensate for a lack of outer and inner closeness - to the personal and to the omnipresent *you*.

Fortunately, these addictive behaviours often resolve, when the courage to dare friendships and closeness is mustered again.

An intervention to transform a dependency pattern

Providing such an impulse to transform self-damaging behaviour is one of the simplest measures in therapy.

Despite that, it can manifest enormous positive effects in the life of the person concerned.

Even if we may never get to know of it.

An elderly patient

To conclude this text, we turn to a patient who was over eighty years old when she came to Cordula's practice because of anxiety attacks, nightmares and ideas of her being pursued by others.

This wealthy **patient** from an aristocratic family had lost her husband many years ago.

A late love
But despite a number of somatic illnesses and her advanced age, she had fallen in love again - 'in her early eighties,' she said with a smile.

Cordula: 'How nice for you! But where do your fears and stalking fantasies come from?
Perhaps you can explain that to me?'

To which **Henriette**, the patient, replied:
'Sure I can - it's my three children and also two of my grandchildren. And it's all because of Walter and me and that we're having a tiny bit of a good time!'

Cordula: 'I see. And what's happening there?'

Henriette: 'Well, we went to Bad Gastein and then to Ischia once, to a nice hotel - but my children won't even notice that as far as their inheritance is concerned.'

Cordula: 'Is that so?'

Henriette: 'Of course. That's peanuts - it really wouldn't matter to them. The foundations of the company have been established by my late husband, who built it up further as the owner.

And the enterprise is still very profitable and has accumulated a considerable fortune over the years, so there is enough for everyone, certainly.

Even if Walter and I were travelling to Mauritius every week! Which, of course, is not our intention,' she added in a cheerful mood.

Offspring on the wrong track
But then her face clouded over: 'And now my children have presented me with this horrible document that I'm supposed to sign, saying that I'm immediately handing the management of my entire business over to them.

And if I don't, they have threatened to have me declared mentally incapacitated!,' she said, while the otherwise distinguished patient shed a few tears.

Cordula was shocked and handed her a box of tissues: 'What sort of children!,' she said involuntarily.
Then she asked: 'And - did you sign this?'

Henriette snorted through her nose:
'Of course not - Instead, I asked them to leave because otherwise I'd have to call security straight away.
That worked.
But they still are my children!,' and with this she started crying again.

Cordula: 'Sure they are. But the most important thing is that you didn't sign this document.

And there are viable solutions for all the other things, including children who somewhat lost their orientation.

But there's one thing still that I don't understand. When your husband died, your children must have received a share of the inheritance, right?
Wasn't that enough for them?'

A life for the company

Henriette: 'Not quite, as it seems. And there are two main reasons for that. To begin with, my husband has passed away at an early age. Then, all our children were under ten and the company still was a smaller business.
And he left the enterprise to me, because he had trained me already to manage it in the future.
Together with a circle of professional advisors.

Our children were given down payments based on the value of the company at the time, which they could use when they reached adult age.
But that was so long ago, I was in my mid-thirties at the time, there wasn't so much to distribute.
That's one reason why they're after me. Because the enterprise has developed well during all those years - but that was an enormous amount of work as well, which meant that I practically was as well as married to the company for several decades!
There even were times when I spent the night in a small room next to the office.
And now the other reason why my children are out to unnerve me:
There's hardly anything left of what they got, because they lived the good life and didn't invest so wisely.

And now they're panicking that I might ruin the whole enterprise - what nonsense!

No - I have built it up over decades, so it would continue to flourish - ultimately for the benefit of our children and their descendants.

But the children themselves didn't show any interest in supporting me, when I was running the enterprise back then - but now they suddenly care a lot about it!'

Cordula: 'So far so good. But your children and grand-children seem to want something from you personally - whatever that may be exactly.

At the same time, I understand the two reasons you mentioned for the erroneous 'financial interest' of your descendants.

One further question in this context: Are your children and grandchildren working themselves?'

Rifts in the family
Henriette: 'Sure - the eldest only has about ten years or so until her retirement.

But since Walter and I are together, they all got this rapture that they might be taken advantage of.

And that annoys me, because I would never do that!'

Cordula: 'Understandable, especially as it's only your decision how you handle your assets.

But apart from travelling together, is there any other financial support from you to your friend Walter?'

Henriette: 'Of course not, he is very particular about that. He used to run a large forestry business and was able to put aside quite a bit. He even insists on paying his share of our travelling expenses, even though I would prefer to invite him.'

Cordula: 'That makes me happy for you - and it speaks in favour of your partner.
Tell me, have your children and Walter had a chance to meet yet?'

An impostor?
Henriette: 'Ha! That's exactly what I've been working on for three years now, ever since Walter and I have got together! But my paranoid descendants don't want to know any of it.
They're just afraid we might get married, which is also complete nonsense, of course!'

Cordula: 'Are you really sure about that?'

Henriette: 'Absolutely. Just imagine, I even asked him once during a very nice holiday, whether a marriage between us would be an option for him.

And what did he answer?
Even if we wanted that with all our heart, it still would be better to let it be.
Because only then, he said, would we keep the chance of making contact between him and my children.'

Blocked information

Cordula: 'Hm! But that's a rather clear statement - do your children and grandchildren know about Walter's attitude? And that your partner isn't accepting any finances from you?'

Henriette: 'I wanted to tell them just that several times already - but then I got so angry at their prejudices towards Walter and finally at this messed up gagging contract with threats of incapacitation that all my sense for such diplomacy disappeared.'

Cheers to diplomacy

Cordula: 'That's quite understandable - and yet it is possibly *this kind of diplomacy*, to use your own words, that seems to be *emerging as a solution* in this family context.'
Additionally, Cordula advised the patient in the following sessions to find a good lawyer for family and inheritance law, just in case. The main focus of co-operation in this brief therapy, however, was to further a reconciliation with the patient's children and grandchildren.

A family conflict that changes the inheritance

Cordula: 'You know, I once heard in supervision about a patient who also had major differences with his children.

And those conflicts were such that it became important to this man to only pass on as little of his considerable inheritance to his children as possible.

In this case, legal constructions were then created with the help of lawyers and notaries, according to this man's wishes, which later on left the children with a minimal inheritance only.

And you could probably do something similar, if your children were going astray completely.

But that's not what you want, as I understand it.'

Henriette: 'No, I don't want that, I want them to inherit normally, despite everything.

But if they give me trouble like that again, I'll tell them the story of this patient that I've just heard from you.

Maybe that will calm the waves a bit.

Systemic Family Therapy according to Milton Erickson
During the sessions, which usually took place three to five weeks apart, **Cordula** sometimes was amazed at the multi-faceted and pioneering spirit of the 'elder lady', as she occasionally referred to her patient inwardly.

Because of the problems with her children, **Henriette** found some of the *hypno-systemic interventions* by *Milton H. Erickson* particularly interesting: 'My children would need a therapist like this Milton Erickson; he might be able to fix it for them!'

Cordula: 'Do you think so?
And what if your children basically just want a little more time and closeness with you?

And regarding **Milton H. Erickson**, I just remembered a story in which two of Erickson's children asked their father to help them.

Specifically, they needed his medical and therapeutic help for two of their classmates, who were struggling with English spelling and had a rather strict teacher on top of that.

So one day, Erickson picked up his boys and their two classmates from school by car.

Before dropping them off at home, he parked the car and had the 'problem pupils' give him their exercise books for English.
He looked through them for a while and then gave them back to the pupils with the strange comment:
'Very good!'

When they looked at their exercise books later on, they realised that they had been corrected all right, but in a completely different way than usual.

Every word that they had written correctly had been underlined by him and sometimes was accompanied by a complimentary comment.

As Erickson's sons reported in the course of time, things slowly improved for the two classmates at school after that experience.'

Henriette smiled. Then she said: 'So you mean . . .?'

Preliminary talks for the good of the family
Cordula: 'Above all, I would like to encourage you to suggest to your children - and perhaps to your grand-children, too - to have preliminary discussions with them under four eyes, to let that old family ice age begin to thaw a little.

These private conversations might help here, not least, because these conflict escalations between you always occurred in a family group setting.
And this development suggests switching to one-to-one conversations for the time being.

A moderated re-encounter of the family
And if steps for a reconciliation can be attained in those talks, I could put you in touch with an experienced family therapist who is able to moderate this common process, while providing therapeutic support, in case you'd want that.'

Eros and intimacy in senior age as well
In addition, **Henriette** sometimes wanted to discuss some topics that she had found in books about *loving intimacy and Tantra.*

'Despite our age, Walter and I are still learning, also in this area,' she said with a wink of her eye that suddenly let her appear at least twenty to thirty years younger.

But sometimes there were also sessions of a completely different kind.
Sessions, in which **Cordula** more than clearly noticed her patient's advanced age.

Facing the curtain
Henriette: 'In all of this, I am of course aware that I am standing in the middle of the threshold towards the other world.
The final transfers of the overall responsibility for the company towards a board of directors are as well as complete.
And there are these last battles in the family.
But also the miracle of a late but heartfelt love, for which I am very grateful!
Still, I would wish for more peace within the family.

But there is this fragment of a sentence that I've found in **Thomas Mann's** *Diary*, which continues to circle in my mind all the while.
It reads, written by Thomas Mann some time after the Second World War and at an advanced age as well:
'Strangely festive rattling away of the remainder of life.'
And that does something to me, because that's partly how I experience it, too,' she added under some tears.

Cordula handed her the box of tissues. After a while, she asked: 'Even if this is ultimately how we're all feeling about our embodied existence - but what do you think could perhaps slow this *'rattling away'* to some degree?'

Go slow with the flow
Motivated by this question, **Henriette** started reading a new kind of books.

She read, for example:
'The Five Secrets You Must Discover Before You Die' by **John Izzo** and besides:
'On Death and Dying' by **Elisabeth Kübler-Ross**.
But also *'Life Lessons'* by **Elisabeth Kübler-Ross** and **David Kessler**.

Finding the way home
In addition, the ways of *mindfulness* and *meditative practice*, which the patient had discovered in the works of **Phyllis Krystal** and **Thich Nhat Hanh**, were topics in their last sessions as well.

This therapy was ended, when a meeting of Henriette's whole family was planned, moderated by the family therapist that Cordula had recommended before.

The New Wild Game

The olden gun still was under the table.
Thinking see me here they' ll never be able!

But then came a wild one, fresh and so brave
As it seemed quite a fine and impressive knave.

He decided with wild ones very like him:
It's best to live shot - now that was his whim.

And they pulled the gun out and then aimed it well -
While sending by this all wildness to hell.

Future aspects in medicine and psychotherapy

The task of medicine and psychotherapy mostly consists in curing somatic and mental illnesses and in alleviating people's suffering; plus saving and preserving lives.

In the field of so-called psychotherapy, which at the same time always requires a near relationship with the body, this task to alleviate and heal can by now be successfully realised in many cases, as we have tried to outline in the case studies in this essay.

The option of Integrative Therapy

By combining analytical, depth-psychological methods with behavioural and hypno-systemic approaches, this is possible in many cases within the framework of an effectively structured and solution-oriented short-term therapy with 12 to 24 sessions.

As the case histories in this book have shown, these are often enabling good results already.

In the field of **Psychotherapeutic Medicine**, however, a real *quantum leap of the results* will become evident in the near future.

This will happen, as soon as the controlled medical use of **Psycho-Active Substances** or **PAS** has been integrated into medicine and therapy again.

IF global peace can still be restored.

And that is a pretty big 'IF', considering these - in early childhood strongly traumatised - and therefore rather egomaniacal global ravings of the delusional, autocratic *Machiavelli Principle* of ageing rulers who, driven by their own fear of - bad, bad! - loss of power and - even worse! - of their personal finiteness, unfortunately are 'capable of any horrors', as the wars and the new arms race of our time are showing so clearly.

Cui bono? Who benefits from the division of humanity?
We should ask ourselves: Who gains by this division of humanity through violence, war and even open nuclear threats? That all of this harms human beings around the world is clear enough.

But who would profit by a Doomsday of the Earth?
Perhaps all the shark families that are endangered by us humans, or maybe the terrestrial tree population?
Or perhaps other, more distant neighbours? -
What do you think?

With some political will - how much past twelve o'clock does it have to be, before things begin to move here? - an **e**vidence-**b**ased **P**sycho-**T**herapeutic **M**edicine, or **ebPTM** for short, which uses appropriate and healing **PAS** or **Psycho-Active Substances** in a controlled way and integrates all useful therapy methods for the benefit of the patients, could certainly make a difference here.

A reminder and part of the 'Take Home Message'
Because this is important for a healthier future for many people and for humanity as a whole, *we are repeating here pages 109 and 110 from before:*

The fact that some of these **PAS** could also be used as *aphrodisiacs to make effective help available* to suffering couples has *so far* hardly been recognised in therapy and medicine.

Psychoactive substances in couples therapy
For instance the **Cannabis** plant, which unfortunately is often 'decried' unscientifically by the medical profession even today, is now proving to be a genuine remedy in many areas of medicine - and for emotionally estranged couples as well.

The mild PAS **Ibogaine** is a natural anti-depressant that can also be of help here in microdoses in the evening.
Ibogaine is freely available in some countries.

The substance **MDMA**, which was used in therapy in the 1970-80s already, then named **Empathy**, or compassion, for group and individual sessions as well as for couples, is even more beneficial for 'healing estranged relations'.
Now MDMA was approved for controlled medical use in Australia in 2023, the first country in the world to dare this important step.
Then approval by the FDA in the USA was expected on August 11, 2024, thanks above all to the tireless efforts of *Rick Doblin, Ph.D.* and the non-profit organisation *MAPS*, which he had founded in 1986.

In the end, however, and despite *two Phase III studies* on successful PTSD treatment with MDMA conducted by MAPS - a panel of alleged 'experts' at the FDA in the USA decided otherwise.

Right in the face of tons of scientific evidence!

So much fear of healing and love. Therefore:

Book *'Alice'* on Psycho-Active Substances in individual, couples and group therapy

Information on the application of *PAS in psychotherapy* is found in our book: *'Alice - through Fire and Water'* and in the articles: *'Peace can be learned!'* and: *'Quo vadis, humanitas?'*; see *Bibliography*.

One more PS in this context:

In the hour lies the power
Almost all tasks
that can be completed in a short time,
can also be fulfilled
in a much longer time.

The healing potential of PAS

This path of controlled medical application of suitable PAS in therapy could fundamentally help many patients, couples and families - as soon as the political will is there to let this happen.

The peace potential of PAS

And if applied worldwide, these PAS would help to make it much more difficult for those severely traumatised, pathologically egomaniac autocrats to come to power in the future.

Because voters, who have gained insight by their own experience, would hardly vote people into leadership positions any longer, who haven't yet experienced PAS for themselves.

This may sound idealistic or utopian.

Nevertheless, the following holds true: People, who had such heart- and soul-opening experiences in a correct setting, are usually no longer starting any fires.

Instead, they help to extinguish them.

End of quote from pages 109 and 110.

Cave! Caution! Both the excessive use and the excessive commercialisation of PAS of any kind carry considerable risks that must be avoided!

All relevant PAS are **generics**, or, in other words, patent-free substances.

PAS in end-of-life care as well

For this, we **quote** from our **book: *'Alice'*, p 291-293:**

Dear readers,

As we are now rapidly reaching the 'Have a good time!' section of this book, here is some further information that might be useful on your way.

Additional indications for PAS in medicine and therapy?

While reading this book, you have seen already that MDMA - and other **PAS** or **P**sycho-**A**ctive **S**ubstances - can be helpful tools in medicine and psychotherapy to treat difficult cases of PTSD, or Post-Traumatic Stress Disorder - and also, that certain PAS can be pivotal in improving and healing the disturbed or frozen intimacy of stressed and suffering couples.

As impressive as the results in these difficult situations may be - there even are other possibilities as well!
And why is that now?

Because we often not only have 'Fear of Flying' - which means that we sometimes are afraid of close and loving intimacy - but frequently we are also affected by 'Fear of Dying', of shedding our mortal coils.

And we find this latter case at the end of many people's lives, for example in palliative medicine, pain therapy, geriatric medicine, oncology and hospice medicine.

You may know already that several healing **VEP-Delics**, or **V**isionary and **E**mpathogenic **P**syche-**Delics** - such as LSD, psilocybin, mescaline, DMT and MDMA - have been administered successfully in such cases in several recent studies - for example in the *LSD study** by **Peter Gasser** in Switzerland.

There, some terminally ill cancer patients were given either a therapeutic LSD dose - or a very low placebo LSD dose - for a longer therapy session.
*Comparable studies have also been done with psilocybin in recent years; see for example:
Michael Pollan: *'How to Change Your Mind'*.

And the result: Most of these extremely ill and dying patients, who had received a therapeutic dose of LSD not only lost their 'Fear of Dying' during this treatment.

Because often they even were able to clarify and resolve old conflicts with family members or friends - which made it much easier for them to face the approaching 'discarding of their mortal coils' with a more peaceful composure.

If you are interested, here is the summary of a similar case, in which MDMA was used to help a well over ninety years old, partially demented woman, who had developed severe anxiety and aggressions towards her family members.

A peaceful mending and dying experience with MDMA
When this situation became intolerable, this woman's son decided to give her an MDMA tablet one evening in a private setting.
The effects of the MDMA experience, combined with the old patient's caring, singing and music-making family, brought about a complete turnaround in the previously extremely hostile elderly lady, who suddenly was able to speak with her children and grandchildren again. -
On top of that, she could even sing along with them!

The best outcome of her *empathy experience*, however, was that this woman remained open and kind towards her family members for the remaining seven months of her life; months that were made so much more precious to this elderly and suffering patient through her catalytic *'Empathy'* treatment with **MDMA** - and by the love of her attentive and caring family.

If you want to read the full story on this case, you can visit **Ralph Metzner's** *Green Earth Foundation* website.
'A peaceful mending and dying experience with MDMA' was published there.
In the Newsletter of May 2nd, 2013, under the title:
'A Peaceful Dying Experience with MDMA'

End of **quote** from our **book**: *'Alice'*, p 291-293.

Does all this make sense?
Yes, it could, as soon as the political will is there to re-integrate healing PAS into medicine and therapy.
Just one last question before we say good-bye:
When are we happy?
As we are running, cycling or breathing?
Whoever finds the right answer - there can be one only - wins a journey into the present!

Heal the Dream!
And this development is instrumental, if we still want to Heal our Dream. Which Dream is that now?
It is the common dream of a life in freedom, equality and democracy, like the American Dream, but not only.
It is the dream of a humanity that has found peace and cooperation between its various groups and nations and with its natural environment, 'our' planet Earth.
If we want to give our descendants on this Spaceship Earth a real chance for the future, then this might be it:
Heat the Dream! Oh-oh - a typo; excuse us.
Rather, it should read: *Heal the Dream!*

Acknowledgements

Now we would like to use this opportunity to thank the people who have contributed over the years towards making this essay on psychotherapy possible.

First, our thanks go to the many patients and clients who have shared their stories and feelings with us in groups and in family, couple and individual sessions, while they often discovered new perspectives and viable solutions for their life at the same time.

It was only this exchange over many years that step by step enabled us to develop the therapeutic approaches and tools presented in this text.

And we are grateful to our beloved parents and families, who faithfully provided us with 'training camps' and 'sparring partners' who, despite occasional hardships and problems, ultimately prepared us in an ideal way for 'real life'.

Similarly, we are feeling deep gratitude to our teachers, mentors and role models at school, in the university and at work.

Colleagues and scientists, whose personal influence or life's work have inspired this *Heart Therapy Blog* have been mentioned in the text already or can be found in the *Bibliography*.

One American psychiatrist, who has strongly influenced our work, although we have never met him personally, is **Milton Erickson**, the pioneer of systemic hypnotherapy, who at the same time often reminded us a bit of the narrative presence of a *Mark Twain*.

Erickson reached us by way of his *'Collected Papers'* and through the films that show him at work, but above all via his direct students, some of whom we were able to meet in person.

For example *Sidney Rosen, David Cheek* and *Jeff Zeig*.

And in addition to Erickson himself and his American students - including **Jay Haley** and his incomparable *'Uncommon Therapy'* - we would also like to thank two German colleagues who had had the opportunity to learn from Erickson directly.

These are our esteemed friends and mentors, *Hans-Ulrich Schachtner*, who had been, p. 120, the *'colleague behind the curtain'*, and *Gunther Schmidt*, who, p. 19, formed the concept of the *'Inner Family'*.

And we are just as grateful for the many years of further training in hypno-systemic family therapy with these influential role models as we are for the methods of **humanistic psychology** and *psychotherapy* that we could integrate into our work in the course of time.

Finally, our thanks go to **Bert Hellinger** for the kindness and wisdom of his family constellations, then further to **Dirk Revenstorf** for his empathic hypnotherapy and to **Arthur Janov** for discovering the worlds of emotions in a new way.

Yet from beginning to end: Thanks always for gratitude.

remember

*Whatever we find
has been designed
by the divine.*

The authors

Gabriele Breucha has a Diploma as an Oecotrophologist Dipl. Oec. troph. or Nutritional Scientist and is a licensed Healing Practitioner and Psychotherapist with her own practice in Munich, Germany.

Anselm Keussen Dr. med./ MD as a General Practioner, specialized in Depth-Psychology based Psychotherapy and is licensed as a Doctor for Psychotherapy, working in his practice in Munich, Germany.

Further books and articles by the authors

Das Meta-Modell der Psychoanalyse - 242 p., 1984 Ger.

Und was macht die Liebe? - 848 p., 2015 German

Alice - through Fire and Water - 360 p., 2018

The Pegasus Paradise - 380 p., 2021

Sathya Sai Baba - 180 p., 2022

Peace can be learned! - 14 p., 2022

Quo vadis, humanitas? - 36 p., 2023

Selected Bibliography

Books on Psychotherapy

Bair, D.: Jung

Bandler, R. & Grinder. J.: The Structure of Magic I and II

Berne, E.: Games People Play;
What do you say after you say hello?

De Shazer, S.: Clues;
Investigating Solutions in Brief Therapy

Erickson, M. H.: The Collected Papers of Milton H.
Erickson on Hypnosis (Ed.: *Rossi, E. L.*), Tome I-IV

Frankl, V.: Man's Search for Meaning - How Frankl, a
young Jewish Austrian Psychiatrist, survived the
Holocaust; Psychotherapy and Existentialism

Freud, S.: The Origins of Psycho-Analysis: Letters to
Wilhelm Fließ, Drafts and Notes 1887-1902;
The Interpretation of Dreams; Studies on Hysteria;
Introduction to Psychoanalysis; Totem and Taboo;
Moses and Monotheism

Fromm, E.: The Art of Loving; To Have or to Be

Goulding, M. & R.: Re-Decision-Therapy

Gruen, A.: Betrayal of the Self

Haley, J.: Uncommon Therapy - Milton H. Erickson's Methods of Hypnotherapy

Hellinger, A. S.; ten Hoevel, G.: Acknowledging what is: Conversations with Bert Hellinger

Hellinger, A. S.: Love's hidden Symmetry

Janov, A.: The Primal Scream

Jung, C. G.: Memories, Dreams, Reflections; The Freud/ Jung Letters; See also: *Bair, D.:* Jung

Jones, E.: Sigmund Freud: Life and Work, Tome 1-3

Kopp, S.: If You Meet the Buddha on the Road, Kill Him!; The Hanged Man; Back to One

Kurtz, R.: Body Centered Psychotherapy

Kübler-Ross, E.: On Death and Dying

Kübler-Ross, E. and Kessler, D.: Life Lessons

Lowen, A.: Bioenergetics

Maslow, A.: Towards a Psychology of Being

Orr, L.: Rebirthing

Painter, J.: Technical Manual on Postural Integration

Rolf, I.: Rolfing

Rosen, S.: My Voice will go with You - The teaching Tales of Milton H. Erickson

Satir, V.: Peoplemaking; Conjoint Family Therapy

Schnarch, D.: Passionate Marriage

Selvini-Palazzoli, M.: Paradox and Counterparadox

Strachey, J.: The Standard Edition of the Complete Works of Sigmund Freud

Smothermon, R.: Winning through Enlightenment; The Man-Woman Book: Transform Love

Watts, A. W.: This is It; Psychotherapy East and West

Watzlawik, P.: The Language of Change; The Situation is Hopeless but not Serious: The Pursuit of Unhappiness

Yalom, I.: And Nietzsche Wept

Books and Media on Psycho-Active Substances = PAS and their use in evidence-based Psycho-Therapeutic Medicine = ebPTM

Breaking Convention: Essays on Psychedelic Consciousness; www.breakingconvention.org

Diesch, M.: LSD - return to clinical research

Doblin, R.: MAPS = Multidisciplinary Association for Psychedelic Studies; www.maps.org
Doblin, R.: A clinical plan for MDMA (Ecstasy) in the treatment of posttraumatic stress disorder (PTSD): partnering with FDA; *Journal of Psychoactive Drugs 34: 185-194*

Fremont-Smith, F.; Sandison, R.:
The Use of LSD in Psychotherapy

Gasser, P.; Kirchner, K.; Passie, T.: LSD-assisted psychotherapy for anxiety associated with a life-threatening disease: A qualitative study of acute and sustained subjective effects

Hofmann, A.: LSD - My Problem Child

Holland, J. (editor): Ecstasy: The complete Guide

Huxley, A.: Island; Brave New World;
The Doors of Perception; The Perennial Philosophy

Kamlet, J.: Ibogaine - ICEERS New York Conference 2010

Lilly, J.: The Center of the Cyclone; The Dyadic Cyclone

Metzner, R.: Green Earth Foundation, where 'A Peaceful Dying Experience with MDMA' was published in the Newsletter of May 2nd, 2013.

Mithoefer, M.: MDMA-supported psychotherapy in severe cases of PTSD (= Post-Traumatic Stress Disorder) First RCT pilot-study; *Journ. of Psychoph. July 19, 2010*

Naranjo, C.: The Healing Journey; The End of Patriarchy

Rätsch, Christian: The Encyclopedia of Aphrodisiacs

Wilson, R. A.: Schrödinger's Cat, T. 2: The Trick Top Hat

Sessa, B.: The Psychedelic Renaissance;
To Fathom Hell or Soar Angelic

Shulgin, A. & A.: TIKAL = Tryptamines I Knew And Loved - An encyclopedic book on psycho-active Tryptamines, like LSD, DMT, Psilocybin, Ibogaine etc.

Shulgin, A. & A.: PIKAL = Phenethylamines I Knew And Loved - An equally huge tome on Phenethylamines, like MDMA, MDA, MDEA, TMA-6, 2C-B, MBDB, Mescaline, DOM etc.

Stolaroff, M.: The Secret Chief - On the Psycho-Active Therapy of *Leo Zeff*

The Global Commission on Drug Policy = GCDP:
www.globalcommissionondrugs.org

Films/ DVD's on PAS = Psycho-Active Substances

Breaking the Taboo

Chocolat

Hope Springs

Hot Frosty

Ibogaine - ICEERS New York Conference 2010

LSD - The Substance

LSD - Drug or Therapy?

The Men who Stare at Goats

Upside Down

WEB-LINKS on PAS and VEP-Delics

PAS = **P**sycho-**A**ctive **S**ubstances
VEP-Delics = **V**isionary and **E**mpathogenic **P**syche-**Delics**

www.maps.org

www.tdpf.org.uk

www.globalcommissionondrugs.org

www.erowid.org

www.breakingconvention.co.uk

www.bluelight.org

www.heffter.org

www.beckleyfoundation.org

www.thc.guide

www.horizonsnyc.org

www.gaiamedia.org

www.neurosoup.com

www.csp.org/docs

www.realitysandwich.com

Books on Intimacy

Deida, D.: Dear Lover; The Way of the Superior Man

Friday, N.: My Secret Garden: Women's Sexual Fantasies; Men in Love, Men's Sexual Fantasies: The Triumph of Love Over Rage

Gillies, J.: Transcendental Sex

Paget, Lou: How to be a great Lover; The great Lover Playbook

Richardson, D.: Slow Sex

Schnarch, D.: Passionate Marriage

gently*

Row, row, row your boat
gently down the stream:
Merrily, merrily, merrily, merrily,
life is but a dream.

*English nursery rhyme.
Songwriter: Eliphalet Oram Lyte.
The title 'gently' was added by the authors.

Books on Spiritual Living

Anand, Deepak: Love Smile Now
An MBA Professor on Sathya Sai Baba

Barks & Green: The Illuminated Rumi

Baskin, D.: Divine Memories of Sathya Sai Baba

Castaneda, C.: The Eagle's Gift; The Fire from within;
The Power of Silence

Confucius: Analects

Daskalos/ Stylianos Atteshlis: The Esoteric Teachings

Dora, H. J.: Glorious Moments with God - A Police
Superintendent of India on Sathya Sai Baba

Field, R.: The Alchemy of the Heart

Galeone, P.: Padre Pio - My Father

Ganapati, R.: Baba: Sathya Sai - Tome 1 & 2

Griffiths, B.: The Marriage of East and West

Gokak, V.: Sai Baba: The Man and the Avatar

House, A.: Francis of Assisi

Kasturi, N.: Sathyam Sivam Sundaram - Tome 1-5 - Biography of Sathya Sai Baba until the mid-1980ies; Loving God - An autobiography of Prof. N. Kasturi, mainly depicting his life with Sathya Sai Baba

Krishnamurthi, J.: Talks in India 1948-1950 - in French: De la Connaissance de Soi

Krystal, P.: Cutting the Ties that bind; Monkey Mind

Lao-Tzu: Tao Te Ching

Levin, H.: Heart to Heart; Good Chances - Meetings with Sathya Sai Baba

Markides, K.: The Magus of Strovolos - see *Daskalos*

Mazzoleni, M.: A Catholic Priest meets Sai Baba

Mittelsten-Scheid, D.: In the Mirror of Silence

Murphet, H.: Sai Baba: Man of Miracles

Sai Baba, S.: Sadhana; The Lamp of Love; Upanishad Vahini; Prema Vahini

Sandweis, S. H.:
Sai Baba, The Holy Man and the Psychiatrist

Shankaracharya, A.: Tattva Bodha - The Knowledge of Truth; Viveka Chudamani - The Crest Jewel of Discrimination

Steindl-Rast, D.: A Listening Heart

Tagore, R.: Fireflies - Poems

Werfel, F.: Star of the Unborn

Wilber, K.: Grace and Grit; One Taste

Yogananda, P.: Autobiography of a Yogi

Yukteswar G.: The Holy Science

closure

*We're incomplete
but yet divine.*

Om

Shanti

Shanti

Shanti